Once
Upon a
Winter's
Heart

# Once Upon a Winter's Heart

## MELODY CARLSON

**CENTER
STREET**

New York  Boston  Nashville

Copyright © 2014 by Melody Carlson

Center Street
Hachette Book Group
237 Park Avenue
New York, NY 10017

www.CenterStreet.com

Printed in the United States of America

RRD-C

First Edition: January 2014

10 9 8 7 6 5 4 3 2 1

Center Street is a division of Hachette Book Group, Inc.
The Center Street name and logo are trademarks of Hachette Book Group, Inc.

The Hachette Speakers Bureau provides a wide range of authors for speaking events. To find out more, go to www.HachetteSpeakersBureau.com or call (866) 376-6591.

The publisher is not responsible for websites (or their content) that are not owned by the publisher.

Library of Congress Control Number: 2013954172

ISBN 978-1-4555-2811-0 (pbk.)

# Chapter 1

"Romance is officially dead," Emma Burcelli proclaimed as she reached for the last empty crate. She pulled off the lid and dropped several pairs of jeans into the plastic box, packing them down.

"That is so coldhearted." Lucy frowned as she handed Emma a small stack of wool sweaters. "Why would you say that?"

Emma looked sadly at her roommate—her soon-to-be ex-roommate. "Because my grandparents were the last of the true romantics and now my grandfather is gone." She let out a long sigh. "I honestly don't know what my grandmother will do without Poppi. Those two were inseparable. I doubt they ever spent a night apart."

"How old is your grandmother?" Lucy handed her the plastic lid.

"I think she's eighty-six now." Emma snapped the lid into place. "They just celebrated sixty-five years last summer. And they both seemed in such good health...I felt certain they'd make it to their seventieth anniversary." Emma stood. "But now Nona is having some health problems, and today she forgot to take her blood pressure meds. My mom's predicting Nona won't last long on her own. I've heard it's not so unusual, I mean, when a couple has enjoyed such a good marriage, that one partner follows the other within the year."

"I'm sorry about your grandfather." Lucy shook her head.

"And that's why I need to go. Nona was like a second mom to me when I was growing up, when my parents were so busy with their careers. I couldn't forgive myself if she passed on too without me getting to spend some time with her." Emma set the last crate onto the stack by the door. "But I hate leaving you in the lurch like this, Lucy. Are you sure you can find someone to share the apartment?"

"I already told you it's okay, Em. Family is important—you need to go. And there's always someone at work looking for something in the city. If I get a girl in here right away I can reimburse you for February."

Emma hugged Lucy. "Thanks for being so understanding."

"Let me help you get this stuff down to your car." Lucy picked up a crate.

After several trips, the compact Prius was packed to the gills and it was time to go. Emma gave Lucy one last hug, blinking back tears. "I'm gonna miss you, Lucy."

"Me too." Lucy's eyes filled. "You better get out of here if you want to beat the commuter traffic."

"Yeah, and I want to get home before dark." Emma got into her car and, giving the old apartment complex one last glance, she waved to Lucy. Really, she reminded herself as she backed out the car, she was overdue for a change. She'd enjoyed her time in Seattle...at first...but these last couple of years had been nothing but disappointing. And she would not miss her job at all. Selling badly illustrated, poorly written, and overly sentimental e-cards was not the career she'd dreamed of while securing her degree in marketing. It was not what she'd signed on for when she'd joined the so-called up-and-coming Seattle marketing firm. They called themselves BrightPond, but DullPond would better describe that company and the "boys" who ran it.

As Emma drove down the freeway she tried to distract herself from feeling blue about Poppi by listening to the radio. But when an Adele heartbreak song started to play, she turned it off and let out a loud sigh. Okay, she knew it was somewhat cold and hard to go around proclaiming that romance was dead, but that was exactly how she felt inside. Not only because Poppi had died, although that placed a definite exclamation mark on her opinionated statement, but also because of her own personal experiences. Too many times she'd discovered that men like her grandfather were all but nonexistent. Truly Poppi had been the last of a dying breed.

Of course, she knew that Poppi would probably argue this with her. He would launch into a passionate lecture about how love was alive and well for those who were willing to take notice. "Just open your eyes," he would often say to people, "love is all around you." But Emma had never been able to see it. Poppi had been lucky in the romance arena. He'd met Nona, the love of his life, in Napoli shortly after World War II—the war that had devastated much of Italy. But despite losing family and suffering deprivations, they'd managed to hold on to this wonderful sense of optimism and hope and love. Shortly after marrying, they immigrated to America, starting new lives in Seattle near some of Nona's relatives. Later on they moved their little family to a small

town in the mountains, and they opened a bookstore in the
1960s.

Her grandparents' story had always sounded so romantic
to Emma as she was growing up that for years she believed
something that wonderful and magical would happen to
her...someday. In fact, she had fully expected it. But after
more than a decade of disappointing relationships, most of
which she preferred not to remember at all, Emma had grown
seriously jaded about love and romance...and men in general. Most of the men she'd dated had proven to be self-
absorbed, shallow, and immature. Whether it was just bad
luck or bad choices, she'd eventually grown weary of dating
in general. And over the years she'd become increasingly certain that good, decent, chivalrous men, like an endangered
species, no longer existed in the real world. True romance was
only to be found in old movies and classic books.

Even Emma's parents seemed to have missed out in the love
and romance department. For as long as Emma could remember they'd bickered and fought over almost everything. The
fact they were still together probably had more to do with the
image they liked to maintain than real love. With highly visible careers, her parents thrived on keeping up appearances.
Although they shared the same building on Main Street, with
her dad's law practice on the first floor and her mom's design
firm up above, anyone who knew Saundra and Rob Burcelli personally knew that this couple lived very separate lives. And anyone who knew them really well, like their close relatives, knew
that Rob and Saundra slept in separate bedrooms. Emma's
mom claimed it was due to Rob's snoring, but Emma knew better. And, really, it wasn't all that surprising. For as long as she
could recall Emma had known and accepted that her parents'
marriage was nothing like Nona and Poppi's.

Tired of these depressing thoughts, Emma turned the radio back on. Even listening to sad love songs was preferable to getting bummed out like this. But now that she was off the freeway and heading into the foothills, the Seattle station was breaking up. Plus it was starting to rain. Turning off the radio, she knew it was time to focus on her driving. At these elevations and this time of year, it could be icy out here.

It was just getting dusky when she pulled up to Nona's house. The familiarity of the Craftsman style home glowing in the rosy twilight welcomed Emma just as it had always done. Despite the frosty air, the bungalow's windows seemed to promise golden warmth and respite and love. How many times had she and her younger sister arrived at this haven in search of refuge? Only now . . . things had changed. Poppi was gone.

She swallowed against the lump in her throat as she parked in front of the house. But as she got out of the car, she was slightly taken aback by the sight of her mother's late model Cadillac in the driveway. What was she doing here at this time of day? As Emma hurried up to the house, she grew worried. Had Nona's health gotten worse? Her mom had mentioned that Nona had neglected to take her blood pressure medicine yesterday. What if she'd suffered a stroke or heart attack today? It was bad enough that Emma hadn't been able to say goodbye to Poppi. But what if Nona was gone as well?

She ran up the porch steps and, knocking on the door, waited a moment before testing to see if it was locked, which would be highly unusual. Then Emma let herself in. "Nona?" she called softly. "Hello? *Mom?*"

"Oh, there you are." Saundra Burcelli rushed toward her, smelling like Obsession perfume and looking typically elegant in her pale blue cashmere sweater set and freshwater pearls. She held her arms open and hugged Emma. "Welcome home, darling. Did you have a good drive?"

"Yes," Emma said quickly. "Is Nona okay?" She peeled off her parka, glancing anxiously around the living room. Everything looked pretty much the same. Except that Poppi's recliner was sadly empty. She turned away, unwilling to break into tears again.

"Nona is fine. I made sure she took her medicine today. And she's resting right now." Her mom tipped her head toward the closed bedroom door on the other end of the living room. "It's been a long day for her. Tending to arrangements for the memorial service and all that. I told her that I could handle it for her, but she insisted on being involved with every last tiny detail. She wants everything to be just perfect for Poppi."

"I got here as quickly as I could." Emma hung her parka on the hall tree by the door. "And I can help her with everything that needs doing from here on out, Mom."

"I'm still surprised they let you off work in the middle of the week like this, Emma. And with such short notice." Saundra peered curiously at her. "I was under the impression you worked for some horrible slave driver."

"As a matter of fact, my boss refused to let me take time off." Emma stuck her chin out defiantly. "And so I quit."

"You *quit*?" Her mother's blue eyes widened in alarm.

"I've hated working there almost from the get-go." Emma lowered her voice and moved away from her grandmother's bedroom door. "I've been considering leaving them for over a year now."

"But in this economy, Emma? Can you really afford to do that?"

Emma shrugged. "I wanted to be free to help Nona. But not just for a week like you suggested. Now I can stay as long as she needs me. I'll help her with household chores and I can drive her to appointments and to the grocery store and whatever—just like Poppi used to do. And I can help with the bookstore too."

"Yes..." Her mom sounded doubtful. "And I'm sure she'll appreciate all that. But don't forget Virginia and Cindy still work at the bookstore."

"I know, but without Poppi around to manage things... well, the bookstore might suffer."

"But I don't like to see you sacrificing your career for—"

"My career was sacrificing itself." Emma ran her finger through some dust on the mantel. "That marketing firm was going absolutely nowhere, Mom. And I was going nowhere with them. I needed a break...a chance to regroup and refocus. You know?"

Saundra made an uncertain nod. "If you say so."

"What's that smell?" Emma sniffed the air. "Is something burning?"

"*Oh, fiddlesticks!*" Her mom turned to the kitchen. "I was attempting to make us some dinner and I completely forgot to—"

"You're cooking?" Emma tried not to sound too alarmed as she followed her mom through the dining room and into the kitchen.

Saundra bent to open the oven door, using a dishtowel to wave away the smoke now billowing out. Meanwhile Emma turned on the exhaust fan over the stove and peered down at what looked like a blackened animal of some kind. "What is it?" she asked.

"It was going to be roasted chicken. But I forgot to turn

the timer on to remind me to turn the temperature down.
It was only supposed to be that high for five minutes." She
scowled at the clock. "It's been at least forty-five."

"Oh..." Emma grimaced. "Is there any saving it? Maybe
we could peel off the burnt layer and—"

"No." Her mom shoved the forlorn bird back into the oven
and, firmly closing the door, she turned off the oven. "Fortunately we have lots of casseroles and other dishes in the fridge.
Everyone has been very generous with your grandmother. I
just thought it would be nice to have a roasted chicken, *that's
all.*"

"Maybe I should take over from here," Emma suggested.
"I mean if you need to go home and fix Dad's dinner. Or do
you ever do that anymore...I mean cook at home?" Emma's
mother had never been into cooking, but even so she usually
ate dinner with Rob.

"I know what you're thinking, Emma Jane. But it may interest you to know that my cooking skills have improved of
late. I even took a French cuisine class at the community college last fall." Her mom patted her platinum blonde hair into
place as if she were getting ready to pose for the cover of a
new cookbook.

"*French* cuisine?" Emma frowned as she reached for a dish-
cloth. "What's wrong with learning to cook Italian food?"
Emma had grown up hearing her father bemoaning the fact
that his wife refused to learn how to make the simplest Italian
dishes. Saundra Burcelli couldn't even make decent spaghetti.
Of course, her mom's usual reaction to her dad's complaints
was to angrily tell him if he wanted Italian food, he could go
to his parents' house to eat. And sometimes he did, because
everyone knew that Nona always had something delicious
bubbling away in her little old-fashioned kitchen.

Her mom scowled. "What's wrong with French cuisine?"

"Nothing." Emma glanced around the messy kitchen. Hopefully Nona hadn't seen it like this. Was all this chaos the result of her mother's attempt to simply roast a chicken? "But, really, Mom, if you need to go home and take care of—"

"I do not *need* to go home," her mom said sharply.

"Okay…" Emma started clearing the counters and straightening the kitchen, all the while wondering why her mother was in such a foul mood right now. Certainly, she was sad over Poppi's sudden demise… but then so was everyone.

"As a matter of fact, I do not plan to go home at all," her mother abruptly declared.

Emma paused from wiping the countertop. *"Wh-what?"*

Saundra turned away from Emma. Fussing with the old spice rack, she meticulously turned each little jar to face out. "I wasn't certain you were coming, Emma," she said slowly. "So I have, uh… well, I've made plans to stay with Nona for a while myself."

"But I *told* you I was coming—and that I'd be here this evening." Emma dropped the dishrag into the sink and placed a hand on her mother's shoulder, forcing her to turn around, face to face. Locking eyes with Saundra, Emma was determined to get to the bottom of this. "You *knew* that, Mom. So why are you acting like you didn't? Or that you need to be here when you knew I was on my way? What's up?"

Her mother looked uneasy as she fingered her pearls, pressing her lips tightly together as if trying to come up with an appropriate answer.

"What is going on, Mom?" Emma studied Saundra closely… something was not right.

"Nothing's going on." Saundra looked down.

"I can tell something's wrong. What is it?"

Saundra folded her arms across her front with a stubborn look.

"Does this have to do with Dad?" Emma demanded. "Did you guys get in a fight?"

"Fine. If you must know, *I've left your father.*"

*"What?"* Emma blinked. In all the years...all the fights...her mom had never left her dad before. Not that Emma knew of anyway.

"You heard what I said, Emma. I've left him. I'm finished. I'm done." Her mother's lower lip trembled slightly as she reached for a tissue from the box that Nona always kept on top of the old refrigerator.

"But why?"

*"Why?"* She looked at Emma with teary eyes. "Because— because it's over—that's why. And please, do not tell Nona about this. She is already stressed over losing Poppi and there's her blood pressure to consider. I don't want her to find out that her only son is a miserable excuse of a husband—not to mention a cad." And now she turned away and hurried from the room.

Emma just stood there feeling dazed. Poppi had died yesterday. And now her parents' marriage was over as well? Not to mention Nona's health was suffering. What more bad news awaited her? She hadn't heard from her younger sister yet...hopefully Anne and her son, Tristan, were okay—although the recent divorce had probably taken its toll on both of them. Emma shook her head sadly as she opened the old fridge. Perusing the assortment of covered Tupperware containers and casserole dishes, trying to find something suitable for dinner, Emma realized that her family was quickly coming unraveled.

# Chapter 2

"Oh, Emma, *dolce*," Nona exclaimed as she came into the kitchen, where Emma had just finished setting the table. "You're here!"

Emma embraced her grandmother. "I am so sorry about Poppi." Emma choked back the emotions flooding her. Nona looked so old and drawn. Her skin was the color of parchment and her soft white hair had fallen out of her bun, hanging around her face in wisps, giving her the appearance that she was hanging on by a thread.

"Yes, yes...so am I, *cara mia*." Nona continued to hug her tightly. "But he went peacefully, Emma, in his sleep. You cannot ask for a better way to leave this world." Nona released Emma. Now both of them had tears running down their faces.

Nona pulled a lace-trimmed hanky from her cardigan pocket and Emma reached for a tissue. "I can't believe he's gone." Emma blew her nose.

"Yes...but we cannot keep crying like this forever now,

can we?" With trembling hands, Nona used her hankie to blot her own wet cheeks.

"I miss him so much," Emma confessed.

"I know, *dolce*." Nona tucked the dampened hanky back into her pocket. "This morning I called out to him...and then I stopped myself...remembered he is not here." She sniffed.

"It will get easier..." Emma assured her. "In time it will."

Nona nodded, but her dark eyes did not look convinced.

"Mom started to make dinner," Emma explained.

"Ah, yes, the roasted chicken." Nona wrinkled her nose. "Is that what I smell?"

"It got burnt."

Nona just shook her head. "Your mama," she said quietly, "is not such a good cook still."

Emma smiled. "I know."

"But there is plenty of food here." Nona waved to the old Frigidaire. "Everyone in the neighborhood, the church, even the bookstore patrons...they all have been bringing me food. As if I might starve to death." She shook her head then looked around. "Did your mother go home?"

"No. She's still here." Emma was unsure of how much to say.

Nona frowned. "Where is she?"

"I think she went upstairs."

"Why is she still here?" Nona's dark eyes narrowed with suspicion.

Emma just shrugged.

"Something is wrong." Nona lowered her voice. "With your mama and papa. I know it's so. Saundra is trying to keep it from me. But I can feel it in my old bones."

Without saying a word, Emma simply nodded. "I heated

up the lasagna for us," she said lightly. "I think it's ready to serve now."

"Lasagna." Nona sighed. "Poppi loved my lasagna."

"I'll go see if Mom wants to join us for dinner."

Nona's dark eyes flashed with concern again. "Tell your mama that there is no sense hiding anything from me, Emma. I will figure it out...eventually."

Emma gave her a sad smile. "I'll let her know."

"And I will open a bottle of rosé." She sighed. "I think Poppi would like that."

A fresh pang of sadness went through Emma as she went off to find her mother. How was it possible that Poppi was gone?

"Is this about New Year's Eve?" Nona asked her daughter-in-law as they were finishing up their dinner.

Saundra looked down at her empty wine glass, shaking her head no.

"What happened on New Year's Eve?" Emma asked.

"Nothing," Saundra snapped.

"That's right," Nona said. "*Nothing*. You are making a mountain out of a mole hole."

"You mean mole*hill*," Emma said quietly. Nona had always gotten her metaphors and euphemisms mixed up.

Nona waved her hand at Emma. "You know what I mean, *dolce*. Your mother is still having hurt feelings for New Year's Eve—almost a month ago."

"What happened?" Emma asked her mom again.

"Your father humiliated me," Saundra told Emma. "That's what happened."

"Yes, Rob was not on his best behavior," Nona sadly conceded. "And all this time—four weeks later you are still angry at him? What about forgiveness, Saundra?"

"I've given that man thirty-six years of forgiveness."

"That is marriage," Nona patiently told her. "You love each other. You hurt each other. You forgive each other. You move on...always forward." She sniffed. "Until it is over with."

Emma reached over and put her hand on her grandmother's. "You and Poppi had a very special love," she said gently. "I don't think a love like that can really be over with. Do you?"

Nona's brow creased. "Maybe not."

"Well, the kind of love Poppi gave you was a whole lot different than what Rob has given me." Saundra spoke in a wounded tone. "It's too bad Poppi didn't teach his only son how to love his wife better."

"Poppi taught by example," Nona told her. "Maybe Rob wasn't watching. And he makes his own choices. We all do."

"And don't forget there are two sides to everything," Emma pointed out.

"You're blaming me?" Saundra scowled at Emma. "Your father made a pass at Patty Hiatt on New Year's Eve, right in front of God and everyone, and you're blaming *me* for it?"

"Rob had too much to drink," Nona said calmly. "You admitted this to me yourself."

"Everyone had too much to drink," Saundra argued. "It was New Year's Eve."

"Nona's right," Emma said. "You need to forgive and forget...*move on*, Mom."

"I did move on, Emma. I moved out."

Nona pushed her chair back with a weary sigh. "Please, *scusa* me. I am tired." She slowly stood. "I am going to bed now."

"I'm sorry," Saundra said with genuine concern. "I didn't mean to talk about this tonight. I knew it would upset—"

"No, no." Nona held up her hand. "We made you talk about it, Saundra. And it is good for you to talk about it. Get it out into the open. A festering wound cannot heal." She leaned over and kissed her daughter-in-law's cheek. "Forgive him while there is still time," she said quietly. "Because you never know, *cara*. You never know..."

Emma started clearing the table, wishing for something positive or hopeful to say, but coming up empty. Nona came over and kissed Emma's cheek. "Thank you for coming to me, *dolce*." She glanced over at Saundra, who was still sitting and frowning down at her plate. "If your mama stays the night, you will have to share the guest bedroom together."

Emma gave Nona a knowing look. "Well, I can't imagine that Mom will want to spend the night away from her fancy Sleep Number bed that she's always bragging about."

"And that just shows how much you know." Saundra got up, carrying her dish to the kitchen.

Nona's brows arched. "Sleep well, *cara mia*," she told Emma as she left the dining room.

Emma waited until she heard her grandmother's bedroom door close. "Mom, are you really spending the night here?"

"I am." Saundra started running water into the kitchen sink.

"What about Dad?"

"What about him?"

"Does he know where you are?"

"No."

"Won't he be worried?"

Saundra shrugged as she tied on Nona's apron. "I doubt he'll even notice I'm gone."

"*Mom.*" Emma slowly extracted the dish drainer from beneath the sink and, taking her time to arrange it just so on the counter, she literally bit her tongue. It would only make matters worse if she spoke her mind and said something truly hurtful. "Mom...you know that Dad has just lost his father and now his wife has gone AWOL. Don't you think that's a lot to put on a man his age? What if he gets so stressed out that he has a heart attack or a stroke or something?"

"Your father just had a physical before Christmas. According to Dr. Maxwell, he's fit as a fiddle."

"Even so." Emma reached for a clean dish towel. "He must be worried."

"Good. I hope he is." Saundra shook a finger at Emma. "Now don't you go telling him where I'm at—you understand?"

"The games that people play..." Emma removed a clean dish towel from the drawer.

"Do you mind washing?" Saundra wiggled her red glittering fingernails in front of Emma. "I just got a manicure on Monday and I'm not sure how well these gels hold up in dishwater."

Emma handed her mom the towel and moved in front of the sink. "Don't you think you're acting a little childish?" she said as she set the glasses into the hot soapy water, just the way Nona had taught her to do long ago. "Running out on Dad like this? I mean, if you really wanted to leave Dad, why couldn't you have waited until *after* the funeral?"

"It wasn't as if I planned it like this," Saundra admitted as Emma rinsed a glass and set it in the drainer. "If Poppi hadn't died, we probably wouldn't have gotten into the fight in the first place."

"I thought the fight was over Patty Hiatt on New Year's Eve?"

"That's what started it...." Saundra slowly dried the glass.

"And if it's any comfort, I can understand how that would hurt your feelings," Emma conceded as she rinsed another glass. "But like Nona said, that was weeks ago. It's nearly February. Surely if it wasn't bad enough for you to leave him back when it happened, you should be over it by now."

"I honestly thought I was nearly over it, Emma. But this morning, well, your father and I were having coffee just like we usually do before work. And we were civilly discussing Poppi's passing and all that needed to be done today. Because Nona was determined to have the funeral service three days after Poppi's death. Anyway, we were talking and... well, your father had the audacity to point out that his parents' marriage was so superior... so much better than ours had ever been." Saundra set the glass down with a loud clink. "And I'm sorry, but it just vexed me."

"But that's true, Mom. Poppi and Nona's marriage was almost magical."

"Yes, I'm well aware of that. But for Rob to throw that in my face the way he did—and here I've been helping with his mother." She furiously dried the next glass. "And I was barely over New Year's Eve—" She turned to stare at Emma. "And you do recall that Patty's my best friend. At least she *was*. Well, it was just too much. More than I could handle. And I was so angry. And our marriage seemed so hopeless. Really, it's a sham of a marriage. Anyway, it was as if a light went on inside my head. And that's when I decided to leave him and come stay with Nona."

"Did you tell him you were leaving him?"

"No, of course, not."

Now they washed and dried in silence for a few minutes. Emma could not think of a single thing to say that would improve the situation. And, really, she rationalized, if she just left her mom alone she would probably go home, wagging her tail behind her. Emma smiled to herself as she scrubbed a plate—one night sleeping on one of those hard twin beds in the guest room and her mom's Sleep Number bed would be calling to her.

"So how are Anne and Tristan doing these days?" Emma asked, hoping to break the stony silence.

"Well, of course, your sister was devastated to hear about Poppi. And Tristan took it quite hard too, poor boy. You know, despite the wide gap in their ages, Tristan and Poppi had been getting quite close after Gerard left. I keep telling your father he should spend more time with his grandson, but does he listen to me? No, he would rather play golf in his spare time."

"He plays golf in the winter?"

"No, of course, not. You know what I mean, Emma. Your father is always too busy—for everyone."

"Do you think Anne and Gerard will ever get back together?" Emma set a plate in the dish drainer. "I mean they were married all those years. I would think that would mean something."

"Don't forget it was a marriage of convenience. If Anne hadn't been pregnant, I doubt they would've married at all."

"But Anne was in love with Gerard."

"She was so young, Emma. Eighteen is far too young to know who you are or what you want out of life. Even Anne admits that she outgrew Gerard."

"But he's Tristan's father and that alone should count for—"

"Really? What kind of father insists on moving his wife and child halfway around the world to some—"

"Florida isn't exactly halfway around the world, Mom."

"It is to a nine-year-old boy who has friends and family right here."

"He would've made new friends."

"And family?" Saundra's brow creased. "Or doesn't that amount to anything?"

"Well...think about it, Mom. His great-grandpa just died. His grandparents seem to be headed for divorce court and—"

"You were always such a pessimist, Emma."

"A realist." Emma set a bowl into the drainer with a thud. "Why don't I finish this up, Mom? I know you've had a busy day helping Nona and plus there's the stress with Dad. You're probably exhausted."

Saundra hung her towel over the chrome towel bar. "Thank you, dear. I appreciate that."

Emma glanced curiously at her mom. "So are you really spending the night here?"

"I told you I was, didn't I?" Saundra squared her shoulders. "I even packed my bags. Come to think of it, they're still in my car. I better get them inside before my new moisturizer freezes out in the cold. At twenty dollars an ounce, I wouldn't want it to get ruined."

"No, no...you wouldn't."

As soon as Saundra stepped outside, Emma grabbed the phone and called her parents' number. To her relief, her dad answered on the first ring.

"Dad," she said quickly. "It's Emma."

"Oh, Emma, are you with Nona now?"

"Yes."

"Is...uh...is your mother there?"

"I don't think I'm supposed to answer that."

"So she is there!"

"Don't say you heard it from me."

"I tried her cell, but she's got it turned off."

"I'm not surprised."

"How long does she plan to stay?" he asked.

"Indefinitely...or so she claims."

He chuckled.

"You think this is funny?" Emma demanded.

"No...not at all. But I know your mother. She won't last more than one night on those old twin beds. Trust me."

"Yeah, I had the exact same thought. I wouldn't be surprised if she goes home in the middle of the night, Dad."

"Don't tell her I know she's there, okay?"

"Why not?"

"Let's just say she's made her bed...let her lie in it." He chuckled again.

"What about you?" Emma asked. "Don't you have to take responsibility for some of this too?"

He let out a long sigh. "I've been taking responsibility for *all* of it...for a long time now, Emma. Maybe your mother is right. Maybe we do need a break from each other."

"Really?" Emma peered out the window to see her mom unloading bags from the trunk. From the size of the pile, it looked as if she was setting out for a two-week vacation or longer.

"Don't sound so sad, Emma."

"But you have so much history...all those years...your family...your image in the community...doesn't it matter?"

"Sure, it matters. But I got to thinking, honey...after I heard the news about your grandpa...I got to thinking about my parents' marriage and how happy they were together. And the truth is I've always felt a little envious. More than a little envious."

"Then why not follow their example?"

He let out another long sigh. "I wish it were that simple, honey."

Emma heard the front door open. "I think Mom's coming in," she whispered.

"Don't tell her," he said quickly. "And I'll talk to you tomorrow...at Poppi's service."

Emma hung up the phone and returned to the dishes. It used to bother her that Nona didn't have a dishwasher; now she thought it was kind of sweet and comforting. Taking time to hand wash the dishes slowed life down a bit...gave a person time to think and reflect. She carefully stacked the pretty Franciscan ware dishes in the glass-fronted cabinet. The pattern was called Desert Rose. As a girl Emma had always thought it sounded like such an exotic name—a desert rose seemed so far removed from their small town in the foothills of the Cascade mountain range.

Emma ran her finger over a raised pink flower on a teacup before she closed the door. Emma had always loved the cheerful dishes and Nona had promised to give them to her when she got married. Like that was ever going to happen. Emma closed the cabinet door and sighed. And, really, it wouldn't seem like Nona's house without these familiar plates gracing the old dining room table. Perhaps it was all for the best after all.

# Chapter 3

Once Emma got her car unpacked, stashing most of her things in what used to be Poppi's library but now looked more like a storage room, she tiptoed up the stairs to peek into the guest bedroom.

"Oh, there you are." Saundra peered up over her reading glasses. With several pillows behind her and one of Nona's afghans on top of her bed, she looked fairly comfy and cozy and had a book in her lap. Emma considered pointing out that her mother was in what had always been considered Emma's bed, but knew that would be childish. Instead Emma set her overnight bag on what used to be Anne's bed and the only part of the room that wasn't already occupied with her mother's extensive collection of Louis Vuitton luggage.

"I was unpacking my car," Emma told her mother as she unzipped her bag.

"Is that *all* you brought with you?" Saundra frowned at the small bag.

"No. I brought *everything* with me. Most of it's in Poppi's library."

"Oh..." Her mom's attention returned to her romance novel.

Emma extracted her pajamas as well as her toiletries bag then started to leave the room.

"It's okay, you can change in here." Without looking up, Saundra absently flipped a page. "I don't mind."

Emma rolled her eyes. "Maybe *I* mind."

Saundra glanced up from her book with a furrowed brow. "Oh, yes, I completely forgot. You're the one who hates to dress and undress in front of anyone." She chuckled. "My self-conscious child."

Emma forced a stiff smile. "Excuse me for not being an exhibitionist like my mom and sister." Emma tried not to feel irked as she went down the hall to the bathroom. But, really, she had not counted on being roommates with her mother tonight. She peeked curiously into Nona's sewing room, wondering if she could possibly set up camp in there since it used to have a hide-a-bed, but like Poppi's library, it seemed to have turned into a storage room as well. Perhaps Emma could convince Nona to have a garage sale this spring... clear some of these things out.

In the bathroom, which was just as cold as she remembered from childhood, Emma decided to get rid of the chill by enjoying a nice hot bath in the old claw-foot tub. And maybe by the time she finished her mother would have dozed off and she could go peacefully to sleep. As always there was a bottle of lavender-infused Epsom salts, which, after a good shaking, came tumbling out into the steaming water. This was going to feel good.

As the bathtub slowly filled, Emma brushed her teeth and

put her long curly dark brown hair into a messy bun. She paused to examine her reflection in the medicine cabinet mirror. In some ways it didn't seem all that different from the girl who used to peer into the same mirror as a child. Same wild hair and dark brown eyes, same pointy nose and slightly pouty lips. Thanks to the foggy mirror, the crow's feet she'd recently noticed were not visible. Thirty-two seemed a bit young for wrinkles, and although some of her friends were already doing Botox, Emma was convinced that an "untouched" face had more character. She'd see how she felt about this ten years from now.

Sliding down into the steaming water, she took in a slow deep breath. Yes, she sighed happily as she sunk lower into the fragrant water, this was just what the doctor ordered. She had just leaned back and closed her eyes when she heard the door opening. Grabbing the washcloth to hold over her front, she glared up to see Saundra coming in.

"Sorry to interrupt your bath," she said quickly. "But I forgot to brush my teeth."

*"Mom."* Emma's voice was laced with irritation and sounded as if she was fourteen again. In fact, that was how she felt.

"It'll only take me a minute. And for all I know you could be in here for hours." Saundra turned on the tap at the sink. "Good grief, it's damp in here. Why doesn't your grandmother get a fan for this room? And a heater wouldn't hurt either. Why doesn't she do some modernizations?"

"Because she's old-fashioned," Emma growled. "And this is an old-fashioned house."

"You don't have to get mad."

"Sorry." Emma took in a deep breath. "It's just that I appreciate a little privacy, you know?"

"Yes, yes. And don't worry, I'm not looking." Saundra giggled as she finished brushing her teeth, acting like this was all just a fun adventure. Finally, after she left, Emma knew the bath had been ruined, but out of pure stubbornness she forced herself to linger. Hopefully her mother would be asleep by the time she finished. But before long the water cooled off and she knew it was time to get out.

As she dried and pulled on her pajamas she thought about how much her mother and sister were alike. Neither of them seemed to have a self-conscious or insecure bone in their bodies. And why should they? Both were gorgeous petite blue-eyed blondes, the kind of women that most men paused to admire, and the kind that some women felt threatened by. Not that Anne or Saundra had ever used their looks to lure men from their wives, but if they wanted to, it probably wouldn't be difficult.

However it wasn't just their appearances that were alike. The way they thought and acted was very similar too. As a teenager Emma had secretly labeled what her mom and sister had as PS—princess syndrome. As an adult she suspected she hadn't been too far off. Oh, it wasn't that she didn't love them both—she absolutely did. She just didn't really understand them. She could always relate better to Nona and her old-fashioned Italian ways.

Emma tiptoed back into the bedroom again. This time she was relieved to see that it was dark in there, and, not wanting to disturb her mother, she was not about to turn on a light. However, remembering how the girls always did a spider check before bedtime—the old house was somewhat inclined to arachnids, especially in the autumn—she was tempted to momentarily flick the switch and search the bed. Instead, she threw back the covers and swept her hand back and forth a few times. Hopefully that would scare anything away.

"What are you doing over there?" Saundra asked in the darkness.

"Sorry." Emma slid into the chilly sheets. "Didn't mean to disturb you."

"It's okay. I can't sleep anyway."

"Missing your Sleep Number bed?"

"Hmmm..."

"It's not too late to change your mind, Mom. You could still go home and sleep in comfort and—"

"I am *not* going home."

"Fine...whatever." Emma pulled the covers up to her chin.

"You don't know what it's like being stuck in a bad marriage, Emma."

"No...I don't." Emma sighed. "Did you guys ever consider marriage counseling?"

Saundra made a sarcastic laugh. "Can you imagine your father listening to a marriage counselor?"

Emma considered this. "Maybe."

"Well, I can't."

There was a long silence and Emma was hoping that her mother was falling asleep, but then she spoke up again.

"When I think about being alone in my old age..." Saundra said quietly. "Well, the truth is, it really frightens me. I don't want to be old and alone, Emma."

"Then why don't you work on improving your marriage?" Emma suggested.

Saundra exhaled loudly.

"I'm serious, Mom. You and Dad have been together all these years and, yeah, I know you've had your battles, but it seems like you've got a relationship that's worth investing some energy into. With some work...I can imagine you both growing old together...happily."

"Oh, Emma, I've tried and tried. But most of the time it feels like I'm the only one putting any effort into it. Your father is so old-fashioned when it comes to marriage. He thinks everyone should be like Nona and Poppi were. The little woman cooks and cleans and sews and gardens...and the man does as he likes."

"That's not true," Emma argued. "Poppi always helped Nona with everything. He liked cooking and didn't even mind cleaning. They worked together in the bookstore and they worked together at home."

"That's not how your father tells it. According to him, Nona worked like a slave and Poppi just did as he pleased."

"I spent a lot of time here, Mom. As kids, Anne and I were over here a lot. We both saw Nona and Poppi working together. Poppi never treated Nona like she was his slave. *Never.*"

"Yes. Well, I have to agree. I never saw Poppi treating Nona poorly either." She sighed. "In fact, I often envied their relationship. I never understood why your father and I couldn't have that."

Once again, Emma wanted to remind her mother that there were two sides to this coin, but she knew that would only invite an argument. And the truth was she was just too tired to fight. "I guess it's like I told Lucy today. True love and romance is officially dead now. It will be buried tomorrow."

"Oh, Emma, that is so dismal."

"Dismal maybe...but I'm afraid it's true. Poppi was the last of his kind."

Emma felt like she was having déjà vu as she climbed into the backseat of her mother's spotlessly clean Cadillac the next morning. With Nona in front and Saundra behind the wheel, and the three of them dressed for the funeral, including hats and gloves to honor Poppi's memory, Emma flashed back to when she was six and allowed to go with her mother and grandmother to Great Aunt Maria's funeral in Seattle. Anne had been too young to make the trip and Emma had felt very grown-up to be included that day. Ironically, she felt very much like her immature six-year-old self again…yet at the same time she felt old…and matronly.

The church was packed with well-wishers, and beautiful flower arrangements lined the altar. Everything about Poppi's memorial service, from the music to the photographs that someone had enlarged and placed near the casket, seemed fitting. And it was touching to listen to the numerous people who shared their happy memories about how Roberto Burcelli—the man the whole town knew as Poppi—had influenced their lives. But the speech that most captured Emma's attention came near the end of the service. She'd never seen this tall, handsome, dark-haired man before. He had on a well-tailored charcoal gray suit that Poppi would've approved of, but he looked slightly uneasy as he stepped up to the mic.

"I realize that my history with Poppi isn't as extensive as everyone else. I was only privileged to know him during the last three years," he began. "But I will always think of him as a true mentor. The first day I met Poppi, he challenged me to read what he called 'real literature.' At first I suspected it was a ploy to keep his bookstore afloat." He chuckled. "But as I got to know him better, I realized it was simply because he respected a good book as well as a good mind. Poppi taught me to appreciate both Hemingway and Dean Martin." Everyone laughed at this because it was well known that Poppi loved

Hemingway and believed Dean Martin was the best singer in the universe. "I will miss Poppi more than words can say, but I'm very thankful to have known him these last few years. He was a good man and we were blessed to have him."

Reverend Thomas wrapped the service up with Poppi's favorite scripture, Psalm 23, and Belinda Myers sang "Ave Maria." Then the reverend announced that only close friends and family would be attending the burial service. And just like Nona wanted, the immediate family rode in the limousine that followed the hearse to the cemetery. Nona and Rob and Tristan sat on one seat and Emma and Saundra and Anne sat on the other. No one spoke . . . but as Nona quietly cried, the tears flowed freely for the rest of them too.

The burial service was formal and old-fashioned—just the way Nona had planned it. And after the final words were spoken, Emma's father stepped forward. "Thank you all for coming," he told their family and friends. "We would be honored if you would join us in my home for a buffet dinner." As Rob gave them directions, Emma and Saundra slipped away, catching a ride back to the church with Saundra's assistant, Meredith.

"We need to make sure that the catering crew has everything under control," Saundra explained as Meredith dropped them off. "And you'll pick up the cake at the bakery, right?"

"I'm on it," Meredith promised.

"That was a nice service," Emma said as she and her mom got back into the Cadillac. "I think Poppi would've liked it."

Saundra just nodded.

"I liked what that man said," Emma began carefully, "at the end of the service."

"What man?" Saundra glanced at Emma as she stopped for the intersection.

"I don't know his name. But he was the one who mentioned Hemingway and Dean Martin."

"Oh, that's Lane Forester."

"It sounds like he was good friends with Poppi."

"Yes. They were very close. I'm sure that Poppi was hoping they were going to become family."

"Family?"

"*Anne*," Saundra declared as if this were obvious.

"Anne?" Emma was lost.

"Anne and Lane," she said with exasperation. "Everyone thinks they make a lovely couple. Don't you think so too?"

"Oh...I didn't know...I mean that Anne was involved with anyone."

"Well, she's not actually *involved*. The divorce only became final last summer. I told her it wasn't very dignified to jump into anything too quickly. Not with a young son."

"No...probably not." For no rational reason Emma felt very dismayed and depressed to hear this news about her sister and this man. Or perhaps, she told herself, she was still grieving Poppi and her emotions were not to be trusted. Of course, that had to be it.

As Saundra drove up the hill to her house, she seemed to have a death grip on the steering wheel and, as she turned into the long driveway, her expression looked extremely agitated.

"Are you okay?" Emma asked as Saundra pulled the car into one end of the three-car garage.

"*Okay?*" Saundra snapped as she removed her keys from the ignition and opened the door. "Do you think it's *okay* that your father has not said a single word to me today?"

"Well, I—"

"*Okay* that he hasn't even acknowledged that I've left him? Is that supposed to be *okay*?"

"Hey, you're the one who said he wouldn't even notice you were gone, Mom." Emma suppressed an amused smile. "Looks like you were right."

"I don't *want* to be right." Saundra slammed the car door loudly.

"He *knows* you're gone," Emma reassured her as they went through the mudroom. "He's just waiting until everything is wrapped up today." She patted her mother's back. "Really, don't you think that's the honorable and mature thing to do?"

Saundra seemed to be considering this as she hung up her coat. "Yes, I suppose you're right." She opened the door to the big, recently remodeled kitchen. Everything looked noisy and busy as several young people wearing smart black-and-white uniforms scurried back and forth with various dishes and trays in hand.

"Looks like they've got things under control," Emma observed.

"Looks can be deceiving." Saundra handed Emma an elegant arrangement of irises and tulips. "Go put these flowers in the dining room for me. And then go make sure the bathrooms look decent. There's no telling how your father left things this morning." She lowered her voice, whispering in Emma's ear. "He could be planning to sabotage me."

Emma gave her mother a skeptical look, but saved her response for later. Really, why would her dad sabotage a dinner that was in honor of his own beloved father? She took the bouquet into the dining room, but knowing how picky her mother could be she was unsure of where to set it. After trying it here and there, she finally chose the antique mahogany sideboard. She nestled it behind the shining stacks of dishes and silverware that awaited the guests. Then Emma took a moment to light the white taper candles as well. Shimmering in the silver candlestick holders, they gave the room an old-fashioned elegant feeling that Poppi would've liked...and Nona would appreciate.

Her parents' house was beautiful as usual. Dignified and traditional—pale maple floors throughout, a few well-placed antiques, raw silk drapes, Persian carpets, a cream-colored chenille sofa, and buttery leather chairs. All this with precise spots of elegant color here and there—a handmade vase or embroidered pillow or a piece of modern art. Just enough to infuse life and interest and texture. Pure perfection. And, of course, it had to be perfect because Saundra was an interior designer. She would rather curl up and die than abide in a ho-hum house.

Emma was pleased to see that her dad was not attempting to sabotage his father's memorial dinner. The bathrooms were impeccable. The hand towels looked fresh, and even the toilet paper rolls were full and neatly folded into a triangle—just like a four-star hotel. Emma even checked the large downstairs master suite where her mother sometimes invited guests to toss their coats. The bed was neatly made and everything in its proper place. Her dad might be ignoring his wife, but he was definitely not slacking today.

When she emerged from the bedroom, family and friends were just starting to arrive. Emma took the time to greet them personally, taking coats and things to her parents' room, trying to make everyone feel welcome and at home. And it was pleasant to see people she hadn't spoken with in years, catching up, meeting new spouses and children, hearing their latest news. She kept her personal responses short and calculated, simply stating she was taking a break in her career and sticking around to help her grandmother. Being jobless and homeless at thirty-two felt a bit like failure, and the less they knew about her, the safer she felt.

Emma flitted around, going from guest to guest and help-ing whenever her mother asked, while also keeping a close eye on Nona, who seemed to be nicely insulated by a couple of older women who were also widows. As Emma refilled the punch bowl, she noticed the man who had captured her at-tention earlier coming into the house. He was immediately met and greeted by Anne, handing his overcoat to her with a comfortable sort of familiarity. After that, it seemed that Anne was reluctant to let the handsome man out of her sight. She took him around, introducing him to some family mem-bers. However, she did not take the time to introduce him to Emma. Trying not to feel snubbed, although this oversight did seem odd, especially if Anne was planning on making him part of the family like their mother had insinuated, Emma decided to take a break from all the noise and chatter by going into the sunroom on the other end of the house.

"Hey, Tristan," Emma said as she discovered her nephew sitting in the sunroom with a slightly forlorn expression. "What're you doing in here all by yourself?"

"Just thinking..." His young brow furrowed as if some-thing was deeply troubling him.

"About Poppi?"

Tristan nodded with moist-looking dark eyes.

"You miss him?"

He nodded again.

"Me too." She sat down in the wicker chair next to him, wondering what she might say to make him feel better. "But you do know you'll see him again someday, don't you?"

"Yeah...I know." He looked down at his hands in his lap.

"And you know that he's still here with us, don't you?"

Tristan looked up with a curious expression. "You mean like a ghost?"

She smiled. "Not really like that." She reached for his hand, holding it up in the light. "See your hands, Tristan, they remind me of Poppi."

He stared at his hands. "Really?"

"Yeah. You have those same long fingers." Now she pointed at his face. "And you have the same coloring as Poppi too. Same deep brown eyes and chestnut hair."

Tristan frowned. "But Poppi's hair was white."

"I mean when he was young like you are, Tristan." She pointed to her own hair. "His hair was a lot like mine—curly too." She pointed back at him. "And like yours...when he was a young man."

"Oh..." He nodded like he understood now.

"So looking at you is kind of like seeing Poppi too. I can see him in you." She smiled. "And that is pretty cool."

Tristan's lips curled into a smile. "Yeah. That is pretty cool." Now they tried to think of even more ways they were both like Poppi—everything from loving books and nature walks and Nona's raviolis to feeling shy and socially awkward at times. And Emma realized that her young nephew, who would turn ten in April, really did seem to have some of his great-grandfather's finest qualities...and it was wonderfully reassuring.

# Chapter 4

Emma and Tristan were laughing over the time Poppi had surprised Nona by taking her to the airport with the intention of swooping her off to Hawaii for their fiftieth anniversary, only to discover that Nona would have no part in it. "She was scared to death of flying and airplanes," Emma explained. "Fortunately, Poppi had trip insurance. They went on an ocean cruise instead."

"Good thing she wasn't scared of boats too," Tristan said.

"Is this a private party?"

Emma looked up to see Anne's attractive friend standing in the doorway. "No, of course, not," she told him. "Feel free to join us." She made a nervous smile—as if he was aware of how she'd been stealthily watching him.

"Thanks . . . I don't believe we've officially met."

"Yes . . . but I think I know who you are," she confessed.

"I'm Lane Forester. And I know that you're Emma Burcelli."

"*Aunt* Emma," Tristan clarified.

"Yes." Lane sat down on the couch across from them. "Aunt Emma from Seattle. I'm actually surprised our paths haven't crossed before this."

"Well, I haven't made it home as much as I should've these last couple of years."

"I know."

"You know?" She tipped her head to one side.

"Your grandfather mentioned it a time or two . . . in passing."

"Oh . . ." She sighed sadly to think of how she missed being home for last Christmas. "Well, that's going to change now. I'll be staying with Nona for a while . . . to help out."

He nodded. "That's good to hear. I was worried for her. She'll be so lost without him."

"Yes . . . and she's had some health issues." She wasn't comfortable with how the conversation seemed to be taking a downward dive—especially after trying to lift Tristan's spirits. "I really liked what you said about Poppi at the memorial service," she said cheerfully. "It sounded like you knew him pretty well."

"I felt like I did."

"Tristan and I were just talking about how much we'll miss him," she explained. "But I was telling Tristan that Poppi left pieces of himself with us—you know, things we can remember him by."

"Like my hands." Tristan held up his hands. "Aunt Emma says they're just like Poppi's."

Lane nodded. "I think I can see that too."

"And we have his hair and his eyes," Tristan continued. "Did you know that Poppi's hair used to be just like mine?"

"I didn't know that. But now that you mention it, I can imagine it."

"And I'm sure Poppi left some things for you," Emma told Lane. "Like Hemingway and Dean Martin."

Lane laughed. "That and a lot more too...I hope."

"There you are." Anne came to the entrance of the sunroom now. Positioning herself by the potted palm, she looked sleek and sophisticated in her dark blue satin dress and diamond earrings. She could easily be a guest at a Manhattan cocktail party. Anne shook her finger at Lane. "I was looking all over for you," she told him. "I thought you'd left here without saying goodbye to me and I was all ready to be vexed with you."

"I was just getting acquainted with your sister," he explained. "And we were all reminiscing about your grandfather."

"Yes. That Poppi—he's going to be missed a lot." Anne sat down next to Lane on the couch. Gracefully crossing her legs and smiling prettily, she looked so together—from the top of her blonde French twist do down to her elegant black heels. She was such the picture of perfection that Emma suddenly felt awkward and unstylish in her long-sleeved gray knit dress and worn black riding boots. But instead of wilting away like an unwanted wallflower, she decided to stay put and find out more about this Lane Forester. After all, if he was really her future brother-in-law, she owed it to her nephew as well as her sister to check him out.

"So, tell me, what do you do?" Emma asked Lane. "I mean for a living."

"Lane's the director of KidsPlay," Anne told her. "He organizes all the extracurricular sports in town. From preschool to middle school, he oversees everything from baseball to soccer to basketball." She pointed at Tristan now. "Speaking of basketball, Monica's boys were looking for you. They wanted to shoot hoops."

"Are they already outside?" Tristan asked eagerly.

Anne nodded. "Get your coat, young man."

Tristan took off like a shot and Anne turned back to Lane, tapping her hand on his knee in a proprietary sort of way. "This guy is also heading up the Big Brothers Big Sisters program in town." Her smile seemed laced with pride, as if she were partially responsible for Lane's achievements. And maybe she was.

"We just started the BBBS foundation a year ago," Lane told Emma. "Big Brothers Big Sisters seemed like it could have such a natural link with KidsPlay. I'd noticed there were a lot of young kids in need of some mentoring. I just do what I can to get them together with mentors."

"That sounds like a win-win for everyone," Emma told him. "I'm sure this town appreciates a program like that."

"I'm helping Lane with a special fundraising event this Friday," Anne said with enthusiasm. "We're hosting a benefit show at the gallery—all the art pieces have been donated by Northwest artists and a hundred percent of the proceeds will go to BBBS."

"That's fantastic," Emma told her. "Mom said you're managing the Hummingbird Gallery. I'll bet you're great at it, Anne."

"It's my dream job," Anne said.

"This fundraiser is a real boost for Big Brothers Big Sisters. Not just for the funds it'll raise, but for the public awareness too." Lane smiled at Emma. "You'll come, won't you?"

"Sure, why not."

"I considered postponing it when Poppi died," Anne told her. "But we'd already done all the advertising and it would be so expensive to start over."

"Oh, I'm sure Poppi would understand. He never liked

wasting money either. And I know how costly an ad campaign can be. In fact, I wish I'd known about your fundraiser sooner; I might've been able to help."

"Emma works for a marketing firm in Seattle," Anne told Lane.

"I *used* to work for one," Emma clarified. "I quit."

Anne's fine brows arched. "You quit?"

Emma nodded. "I'm going to stick around and help with Nona for a while."

"But your career...you gave it up?" Anne looked truly concerned.

"It was time for a change," Emma explained. "The firm had some problems. I'm really glad to be done with them."

"Nothing wrong with getting a fresh start," Lane said optimistically. "That's what I did when I took the KidsPlay job here three years ago. A complete change for me, but I've never regretted it. Never looked back."

"Really?" Emma felt hopeful.

"Lane used to work for a big software company in Seattle."

"Oh..." Emma nodded. "I hear that can get old fast."

He chuckled. "Yeah...it did."

"Well, if you need any other marketing help for KidsPlay or Big Brothers Big Sisters, just let me know. I'd be happy to help out."

He grinned. "I will definitely keep that in mind."

Anne stood and, reaching for Lane's hand, tugged him to his feet. "Now before you actually sneak out without saying goodbye, there's someone I really want you to meet." She winked at Emma. "You don't mind if I take him away, do you?"

Emma laughed. "I wouldn't dream of trying to stop you." She watched as Anne, chatting amicably, gracefully guided

Lane back into the mainstream of the house. Emma still didn't quite know how Anne did it. Socially skilled, that girl could maneuver her way into and out of almost any situation with total ease and comfort. Emma had not been blessed with those particular skills. And the truth was, she didn't really care either. Flitting around with all the guests today had been exhausting. And schmoozing had always made Emma want to pull her hair out. Anne could have it.

It wasn't until the last of the guests were leaving that Emma realized she was alone in the house with her two silently feuding parents. The widow friends had taken Nona home earlier, and now Emma needed to figure out a way to escape herself.

"I don't have my car here," she reminded her mom as they were putting the kitchen back to order. "And I'd like to get back to check on Nona. So, if you don't mind finishing up without me, I'll just walk."

"Walk?" Saundra frowned.

"Yeah. It's barely a mile and I could really use the exercise."

"But it's so cold out."

"It's okay. I have my coat and hat and gloves." Emma pointed out a foot. "And these boots are good for walking."

"But I'll be ready to go pretty soon."

"I really want to walk, Mom." Emma kissed her mom's cheek. "See you later." Emma left the kitchen and went out to where her dad was straightening things up in the living room. "I'm going now," she told him. "I don't want Nona to be home alone for too long."

"Thanks for helping out today." Her dad hugged her. "I think Poppi would've liked how things went, don't you?"

"Absolutely. And Nona seemed to appreciate it too."

"Thanks for helping with her, Emma. That takes a load off my mind."

"I'm happy to." Emma nodded toward the kitchen. "I hope you and Mom can talk this thing out now that the funeral is behind us."

He shrugged. "Not sure she wants to talk."

Emma frowned. "Well, I better go. I don't want Nona thinking she's been abandoned." As Emma went for her coat, she hoped that her dad wouldn't figure out that she planned to walk to Nona's. She didn't want to give him any excuse to keep avoiding his wife. The sooner she got out of here, the better their chances for talking this thing through.

She hurried out the front door and down the driveway. The afternoon air was cold and crisp, and she hastened her pace in hopes of getting warm. She hadn't walked this route for years. Probably not since high school, and even then she usually rode her bike. But it felt good to walk today—the cool air seemed to help clear her head. She was just at the foot of the hill when she heard a car pull up beside her. To her dismay she realized it was her mom's Cadillac.

"Hop in," Saundra called out to her.

Emma considered insisting upon walking, but knew how stubborn her mother could be. "Where are you headed?" she asked as she closed the door and reached for the seatbelt.

"Where do you think?"

"Mom," Emma said in exasperation. "Why are you doing this?"

"Because your father is a total jerk."

"Did you even try to talk to him?"

"It's pointless, Emma." Saundra stopped at the stop sign. "And if it's all the same to you I'd rather not talk about it."

"That's fine with me." Emma turned to look out the side window.

"I noticed you talking to Lane," Saundra said lightly. "What do you think of your sister's beau?"

"He seems like a very nice man."

"Yes. We all like him."

"How long have they been together?"

"Together?"

"You know, as a couple...how long?"

"Well, I'm not sure they're officially a couple yet."

"Right..." Emma remembered her mother's concern about Anne's divorce and not rushing into anything. Keeping up appearances.

"Although Valentine's Day is coming up...maybe Lane will ask Anne out."

"Maybe..." Anne wondered how Tristan would feel about his mother dating someone who wasn't his father. "So...why did Gerard and Anne break up?"

"You know as well as anyone, Emma. Gerard took that job in Florida and Anne didn't want to uproot Tristan."

"That's never made sense to me. I mean if you love someone...if you're committed to them...wouldn't you stay together through thick and thin? Isn't that what marriage vows are all about? For better or worse, sickness and health, richer or poorer?"

"You've always been such an idealist, Emma."

"Maybe so...but I don't get why Anne had to be so stubborn about leaving. It seems like she'd like Florida. I mean she loves summer."

"She'd just started working at the Hummingbird when Gerard got offered the job. And Tristan was doing so well in school. He'd had such a rough time in first grade. Besides that, Anne had just redecorated the condo. I completely understand why Anne didn't want to give up everything to move to Florida."

"But I thought the Florida job was just going to be temporary," Emma reminded her. "Just a year or two. I understood that Gerard was being trained by the corporation so that he could work in any insurance agency, including here."

"Well, he's been there nearly two years already," Saundra pointed out. "And it doesn't sound like he's coming home anytime soon."

"That must be hard on Tristan."

"Yes. But he's still got family and his school and his friends and sports. And did you know that Lane is Tristan's Big Brother? They do something together at least once a week. It's really very sweet."

"And Lane's been in town for about three years, right?"

"That sounds about right."

Emma didn't like being suspicious, but she wondered if Lane had anything to do with why Anne had refused to accompany her husband to Florida. Emma had seen the way Anne looked at Lane in the sunroom, the way she'd spoken to him, placed her hands on him...almost as if she was demonstrating ownership. Yes, it probably wouldn't be too long until Tristan's Big Brother became his stepfather. And, really, what was wrong with that?

# Chapter 5

After the second night of sharing a room with her mother and the realization that it wasn't only her dad who snored, Emma started putting together an escape plan. But first she needed to clear it with Nona. "Do you mind if I do some rearranging of the rooms upstairs?" she asked her grandmother as the two of them lingered at the breakfast table. Saundra had already left for an early appointment at work.

"No, not at all." Nona reached for her coffee cup. "I hardly make it up the stairs these days. With you and Anne all grown up, I don't sew. I'd rather knit."

So after finishing cleaning up the breakfast dishes and kitchen, and seeing that Nona had taken her pills and was comfortably settled in front of a crackling fire with her knitting and a good book nearby, Emma went back upstairs. Rolling up her sleeves, she went into attack mode, clearing and cleaning and organizing until she started carving a space for herself in Nona's old sewing room. The hide-a-bed was still sturdy and sound and it actually felt more comfortable than the twin bed she'd been sleeping in.

She took a break at lunchtime to warm some soup for Nona and herself, explaining her progress as they ate. "I hope you don't mind that I stored even more things in Poppi's library."

Nona waved her hand. "Poppi would be glad to know you are making yourself at home, Emma. Do as you please."

After lunch, Nona retired to her room for a nap and Emma returned to her upstairs project. By the time Saundra came home from work, Emma was just putting the freshly laundered bedding on the sleeper sofa and smiling in satisfaction at her progress. The old sewing room was transformed into a cozy-looking bedroom. All Emma needed to do now was to move her things in and get settled.

"Well, well..." Saundra came into the room and looked around. "It's not terribly stylish, but it is less crowded than the other bedroom. Want to flip a coin for it? Or should age come before beauty?" She laughed lightly.

"What?" Emma blinked. "You want this room?"

"Well, I know how much you and Anne loved that old bedroom," Saundra said. "I just assumed you'd prefer it to this one. I can easily move my things in here. I don't mind at all."

Emma was dumbstruck. She looked longingly at the freshly made bed then turned back at her mother and sighed. "Sure, if that's what you want."

Saundra ran her hand over the faded blue floral wallpaper. "You know I could get some of my people in here to do a complete makeover. This space could be quite attractive in just a few days."

"Or you could leave it and call it shabby chic." Emma shrugged. "I'll help you move your things in here." Seeing the spare bedroom, Emma reassured herself it was a fair trade.

This room, with its southern exposure and larger closest, really was better than the old sewing room. At least she could have her bed by the window back . . . as well as her privacy. By the time her mother's things were moved out, Emma was just fine with it.

Although Emma desperately needed a shower after all of today's cleaning, she knew it was time to get dinner started. And by the time she got to the kitchen, Nona was already poking around in the fridge and insisted on helping with dinner. But since they still had food from the generous neighbors and friends, it was mostly a matter of heating some casseroles and setting the table and Nona's company was pleasant in the kitchen.

"How long do you think your mother will be staying with us?" Nona asked quietly as they worked together.

"I have no idea. I honestly didn't think she'd be here this long."

"Saundra can be stubborn." Nona checked on the oven.

"I know." Now Emma confided to Nona about how her mother insisted on having the sewing room.

"After you worked so hard?" Nona frowned.

Emma laughed. "The truth is I like the old spare bedroom better anyway."

Nona nodded, patting her arm. "Yes, yes. It is better. More sunshine."

Tonight the three women dined in the kitchen instead of the dining room. Saundra seemed determined to keep the conversation cheerful and upbeat, making small talk about work and happenings in town. No mention was made of her extended stay or the situation with the bedrooms upstairs.

Then, after dinner as they were clearing the table, Nona noticed the calendar on the fridge. "Oh, no—is it true?"

"Is what true?" Saundra asked.

Nona tapped a crooked finger on the calendar. "Is it *February?*"

"Oh, yes. Today is February first," Saundra told her. "I turned the calendar over for you. Surely, you don't mind."

"Oh...*Mama mia*." Nona shook her head with wide eyes. "How can it already be February?"

"I know what you mean." Saundra set some dishes by the sink where Emma was already running water. "Time goes by so quickly...the older we get."

"No, no, that is not it, *cara*." Nona sat down on the yellow kitchen stool with a loud sigh. "Oh...dear..."

Emma turned around to look at her grandmother. "Are you okay, Nona?"

With her hands over her face Nona groaned. "It cannot be."

Alarmed, Emma hurried over, placing a hand on Nona's shoulder. "Nona, what's wrong? Are you feeling sick?"

"Sick at heart, *dolce*."

"What's wrong?" Saundra asked with concern.

Nona looked up, pointing at the calendar with a dismayed expression. "Poppi would be sad...so sad."

"Why?"

"Because it is February today. And Poppi's Valentine decorations are not yet up. It is wrong. All wrong."

"Oh...I forgot." Emma grimaced to remember Poppi's obsession with this particular holiday. Poppi always decorated the bookstore to the hilt on the first day of February. He'd been doing it for years. As a child, she had loved this tradition. As an adult...well, it seemed a bit much.

"Maybe Virginia and Cindy already put the decorations up...?" Saundra suggested weakly.

"No...no...they have never done it before. They would

not know where to find them or how to put them up. That was Poppi's job." Nona sighed. "Maybe it does not matter...all things must come to an end...someday." She slowly stood. "I am very tired. Very tired."

"Don't worry, Nona, I'll go put the decorations up," Emma said quickly. "I used to help Poppi all the time when I was a kid. I know how to do it."

"Oh, *cara mia*!" Nona grasped Emma's hands in her own. "*Grazie, grazie!* You are an angel!"

Emma smiled. But she was glad that Nona couldn't see through to her heart since Emma's attitude toward decorating for Valentine's Day was anything but angelic. "Don't you worry about it, Nona. The store will be festive and bright before the night is over."

"Ah, for the energy of youth," Saundra said. "All I want to do is put my feet up."

"We will finish the dishes," Nona told Emma as she handed her a set of keys. "You go to the store, *dolce*. It's closed now. No one will be there to disturb you. Hurry, hurry."

As Emma hurried out to her car, she was relieved she hadn't taken time to shower yet. Digging around in the dusty back room, climbing up the ladder and mucking around, it was just as well that she still had on her old blue cardigan and worn gray cords. Thankfully there would be no one around to see her.

It was just beginning to rain as she started her car. Grumbling to herself over the foolishness of decorating for such a silly holiday, she drove the few blocks to town and turned onto a nearly deserted Main Street. The rain was coming down hard now and, according to the readout in her car, the temperature was close to freezing. Perhaps it would turn to snow before long. She parked directly in front of the darkened bookstore, dismayed to see the sad black wreath hanging on the door. Most likely this was Nona's doing. And, really, it seemed more fitting to this time of year and tonight's weather than the garish hearts and cupids she would soon be releasing from their boxes. But, out of respect for Poppi and concern for Nona, she would complete this task.

She quietly let herself into the bookstore, turning on the lights and locking the door behind her. The familiarity of the store warmed her heart slightly. Books were always so friendly, so homey. Perhaps she didn't really want to be the Grinch who stole Valentine's Day after all. She heard the familiar meow of the bookstore cat.

"Hey, Gattino," she called gently to him. "You're being invaded tonight, old boy." He rubbed up against her legs and she bent down to scratch his furry head. "Not just by me either. Before I leave, this place will be crawling with cupids. I hope you don't mind."

She headed for the back room and turned on the lights. She soon found the cabinet where the Valentine decorations were stashed up high. She considered hunting down a stepladder, but thought perhaps she could reach them. After all, she was nearly as tall as Poppi had been, and he never used a stepladder. She stretched up to balance the highest box on her fingertips. She was just easing it down when the whole thing tipped and tumbled and, opening up, cascaded down upon her with a loud crash.

Stunned to find herself sitting on the hard cement floor surrounded by lacy pink hearts and purple flowers and scarlet cupids, she felt like screaming. So this was her reward for trying to be a good sport? All feelings of warmth and goodwill evaporated and suddenly she felt like shredding all these old cardboard cutouts to pieces. She picked up a stuffed white bear holding a red satin heart and maybe it was her, but he seemed to be smirking. Honestly, did Burcelli Bookstore really need this nonsense? Did she have to make the dignified bookstore resemble an advertisement for a totally frivolous holiday? A commercialized occasion that was more about chocolate and roses than it was about true love and romance? Seriously, would anyone really care or even notice if these Valentine monstrosities mysteriously disappeared?

Yes...Nona would care. So would Poppi...if he knew. Tempting as it was to dump all this into the Dumpster out back, she would never be able to live with herself if she did. Emma was plucking a pink crepe paper streamer from her hair when she heard the sound of a door creaking open. At first she thought it might be the cat, but how would Gattino open a door? Holding her breath, she listened.

"*Hello?*" a firm-sounding male voice called out. "Anyone in here?"

She froze, unsure of what to do and wondering where her phone was, then asking herself, *Would a burglar call out a greeting?*

"*Hello?*" he called again. "Virginia? Cindy? Anyone in here?"

The sound of approaching footsteps sent a chill down her spine—and yet if this intruder knew the names of the employees, he probably wasn't about to rob the place, *was he?*

She considered pulling the Valentine box over her head and hiding beneath it, but at the same time knew that was just silly. Although she did glance around to see if there was something handy to use as a weapon—just in case. Perhaps she could whack him with a large book. Still hunkered down in the Valentine mess, she watched helplessly as a man emerged from the shadows back by the employees' restroom.

"Hello?" he called again. "Anyone here?"

As he stepped fully into the light, she instantly recognized him. Although he wasn't wearing the stylish charcoal suit, she knew who he was. *"Lane Forester?"* She stared at him in wonder. "What?"

*"Emma?"* He looked as stunned as she felt. "What are you doing—*what happened?*" He rushed over to help her to her feet. "Are you *okay?*"

"Yes." She brushed off the streamer. "Well, except for feeling pretty clumsy."

"What are you doing here?"

She explained how Nona was so distressed. "Poppi always put the Valentine's Day decorations up on February first." She shrugged. "So I offered to come do it."

He nodded. "That's right. Today *is* the first."

She bent to pick up a lace trimmed heart, dropping it back into the box. "The truth is I'd just as soon light a match to all this than hang it up."

"Really?" He squatted down, helping her to pick up the decorations and replacing them into the box.

"Can you imagine what a glorious bonfire this would make?" She whirled some crepe paper around like a banner.

"It would probably burn fast." His brow creased with concern, as if he thought she was serious.

"The truth is..." She dropped a pair of arrow-connected hearts into the box. "I hate Valentine's Day."

"Wow...that's really sad."

"I'm sorry." She tossed in another cupid. "But I just happen to think it's a dumb holiday."

"Why is that?" He peered curiously at her.

Now even though he was casually dressed in a sweater and cords, she felt like a bag lady in her dirty cleaning clothes.

And her hair—was it still in the same messy ponytail from this morning? Perhaps that's what made her decide to speak her mind. What difference did it make what he thought of her? "Valentine's Day is like a cruel joke," she said as she scooped up some cupids. "First of all, for those who aren't in a relationship, it simply reminds them of their pathetic loneliness. And for couples it's just an excuse to go out and waste good money on fattening chocolates or hothouse roses or overly expensive jewelry. And then, of course, there's always the guilt trip for those unfortunates who forget about the holiday—woe unto the husband who shows up empty-handed. And then there's the hurt and disappointment for the ones with dashed expectations. *Happy Valentine's Day.*"

"Wow, it seems you've given this some serious thought." He set the last of the decorations on top of the box and stood up straight.

She shrugged, wishing she had taken a little more time to clean up now. "Well, I worked in advertising long enough to get a bit jaded about commercialism." She shoved her hands in her pants pockets. "Sorry to be so gloomy. But thanks for helping. Now I better get busy."

"So, even though you despise Valentine's Day, you're still going to put up all these decorations?"

"Oh, yeah..." She reached up for another box. "It's a tradition, you know." She forced a smile.

"Here, let me get that for you." He stepped in front of her, easily lifting it down from the cabinet.

"Thanks."

"Well, this is all wrong." He set the box in her arms then bent down to pick up the larger one from the floor.

"What's all wrong?"

"This bah-humbug attitude over Valentine's Day."

"I know," she admitted sheepishly. "And I do feel guilty for being so negative. I know Poppi would be disappointed in me."

He nodded. "He would definitely not approve."

She turned away now, walking toward the front of the store. She could hear him following her as she went over in the lounge area. It brought no comfort to her to realize that the lighting out here was much brighter than the back room. But why should she care about what her sister's boyfriend thought of her? She set her box down on the coffee table then turned to peer at him. "Hey, how did you get in here anyway? Do you have a key or something?"

"I leased the office upstairs from Poppi. It's the headquarters for KidsPlay. I normally use the outside exit when I work late." He set down his box. "I was just getting ready to leave when I heard the noise down here. I knew the store was closed by now, so I thought I better check it out. I came down the interior stairs."

"Oh..." She picked up a sassy-looking cupid and attempted to straighten its slightly bent bow. "Do you always work this late?"

"Sometimes."

"Well, thanks again for your help." She made a stiff smile as she tossed the cupid back into the box. "I better get busy or I'll be here all night." She glanced around, wondering where the ladder might be hiding.

But Lane just stood there and, with a stern-looking expression, folded his arms across his front. "I'm sorry, Emma, but I think an intervention is needed here." He stepped between her and the boxes, almost as if he was protecting the decorations.

"What?" She frowned at him but then remembered her

threatening words about burning everything. "You don't honestly think I'm going to destroy my grandfather's decorations? I was just kidding about setting them on fire." She forced a laugh. "Don't worry, Lane, I'm not really a pyromaniac. And I won't be torching anything tonight."

"No, I didn't think you would. But just the same I believe you need an intervention. Especially since you're going about this all wrong."

"What's that supposed to mean?"

"I mean you do not have the *right spirit*."

She let out a long sigh.

"And if you can't decorate the bookstore cheerfully, you should not do it at all."

"I know...I know..." She held up her hands in a helpless gesture. "What can I say?"

He rubbed his chin as if thinking. "You're probably not aware that I helped Poppi decorate for Valentine's Day these past couple of years."

"Seriously?" She tilted her head to one side, studying him. "You honestly helped him decorate?"

He nodded. "Uh-huh. Which is precisely why I know you're going about this all wrong, Emma Burcelli."

"So...what do you recommend?"

"I recommend that you go find the ladder, the Scotch tape, the masking tape, the push pins, thumbtacks, and whatnot. Meanwhile I'll go get what's missing."

"What's missing?"

He shook his finger at her. "You take care of your list and I'll take care of mine, Miss Burcelli, and we will meet back here."

It didn't take long to locate tape and pins, but the ladder was another matter. She finally found it tucked behind a shelf in the storage room. She was just dragging it out when she heard music starting to play. That wasn't so unusual when the store was open. But why now? As she emerged into the bookstore, she realized it was Dean Martin. Well, of course—Poppi would approve that. She couldn't help but chuckle as she carried the ladder out to the lounge area. But when she saw Lane standing by the coffee table with a bottle of wine and two glasses—and an opened box of chocolates on the table—she was too stunned to respond.

"I see you found the things on your list," he said as he filled a glass with red wine.

"What on earth are you doing?" She stared at him in shock.

"This is how it's done." He handed a filled a glass to her then filled his own and held it up. "Poppi always started with a toast to—"

"No way," she said. "I helped Poppi decorate all the time and he never did anything like—"

"How old were you the last time you helped your grandfather?"

She considered this. "Well, I was still in high school...eighteen maybe."

"Uh-huh." He gave her a knowing look. "I doubt Poppi thought it was appropriate to serve his underage granddaughter wine. But, trust me, this is how Poppi taught me to decorate for Valentine's Day." He nodded to the comfortable chairs. "Please, take a seat and I'll explain."

Feeling a bit like Alice through the looking glass, Emma sat down.

"You see, the first time I came down here to help Poppi was on a night much like this. Dark and stormy. Your grandfather brought out a bottle of wine and—"

"Since when did he keep wine at the bookstore?"

"I don't know when he started this tradition...but for book clubs and special events...he always seemed to have a few bottles on hand in the back room." Lane gave her a tolerant smile. "May I continue?"

"Please, do."

"So, before we could start decorating, Poppi insisted on pouring us a glass of wine and then he made a toast." Lane held his glass up. "He said, 'To Valentine's Day and to true love.'" Now Lane reached over and clinked his glass against hers. "Come on, you have to say it too."

"To Valentine's Day and to true love?" she echoed with uncertainty. What was going on here? Was this guy for real?

"Very good." He took a sip and, feeling like she was playing a part in a movie or maybe just dreaming, she followed his example.

"Not bad," she said as she tried another sip.

Now Lane picked up the box of chocolates and held them out to her. "And this was the next part of the preparation."

"Seriously?" She stared at the lush-looking treats.

"On your Poppi's honor," he said with a sincere expression.

She hesitantly reached for a chocolate. Taking a cautious bite, she studied him with curiosity. "You're not pulling my leg?" she asked. "Poppi really gave you wine and chocolates and played Dean Martin for you?"

He laughed. "Yes. He told me that he wanted to put me in a Valentine's state of mind before we decorated. He said if you didn't do it with the right spirit, it would ruin everything."

Emma nodded slowly. "Yeah...I actually remember him saying that when I was a girl. But I always had the right spirit back then." She took another sip of wine, savoring it with the flavor of the dark chocolate, suddenly remembering what fun they'd had decorating together. Maybe he had played music.

Lane reached for another chocolate. "Well, the truth is, I was a bit like you when I met Poppi. I wasn't too keen on Valentine's Day either. I suspect that's why he invited me to help him decorate that year."

"Really? You were a Valentine's Day Scrooge too?" She felt unexpectedly hopeful.

"Yep. I didn't believe in true love anymore...long story, but Poppi got me to tell him about it. And Poppi helped me to deal with it." He held up his glass again. "Here's to Poppi."

She clicked her glass against his for a second time. "To Poppi." And as they sat there in the lounge, listening to Dean Martin, drinking red wine and eating chocolates and talking, she wondered if it was possible that romance still lived after all. Perhaps she'd been wrong to declare it dead.

# Chapter 6

By the time they finished decorating, it was nearly eleven o'clock, and Emma thought the bookstore had never looked better. "I don't even know how to thank you," she told Lane as they put the ladder and empty boxes in the back room. "Nona will be so relieved."

"I think Poppi would like it too," Lane said as he flicked off the light switch.

They gathered their coats and turned off the music and lights in the store and were both leaving by the front door when Emma realized that she hadn't had this much fun in ages...maybe years. It was almost like being on a really good date. But even as the thought hit her, it was immediately doused with a heavy load of guilt. Lane was her sister's beau. And because he had been Poppi's good friend, he had come to her aid tonight. That was all there was to it. To imagine anything more wasn't just foolish; it was downright dangerous. And she loved Anne too much to even consider such a thing.

"Be careful out here," Lane warned as she was locking the door. "There seems to be some ice—" And just like that, he was flat on his back.

"Lane?" she cried out. "Are you okay?"

He chuckled. "Well, other than bruising my manly pride."

She reached out a hand to pull him up, but as soon as he grasped her hand, her heel slid on the ice and she went down too—right smack on top of him. "Oh, no!" she gasped, trying to extract herself from his arms. "It really is slick out here." She giggled nervously as she rolled off of him, struggling to get her bearings. "Sorry about that."

"No problem." He laughed. "The rain must've frozen." He sat up and looked around. "It's a solid sheet of ice."

They pushed and pulled and slipped and slid, breaking into uncontrollable laughter, as they tried to help each other stand on their feet.

"It's a silver thaw," Emma said as she held onto the door handle, looking out to a streetlight that was coated in a layer of ice and shimmering magically. "Beautiful . . . but treacherous."

"Far too slick to drive." Lane grasped the side of the building to support himself. "I think we'll have to hoof it."

"Yes, I guess I better leave my car here," Emma said. "Nona's house is only a few blocks away."

"I'll walk you home," he offered.

"But what about you? How will you get home?"

He smiled. "No worries. I live just down the street from you."

"Really? You live on Nona's street?"

"In the old McCormick place."

"Oh, that's a lovely house."

"Do you think we can make it?" she asked as they took some tentative steps, slipping and nearly falling down again.

"Maybe we should think of it as skating," he suggested, "not walking."

"That's a good idea." She imitated how he was sliding his feet.

After a few more slips and falls, Lane suggested they hold hands and help each other as they cautiously skated and slid along the sidewalk. Under any other circumstances, this could be considered very romantic. But Emma knew that it was simply a matter of necessity. And it was slow going.

"It's hard to believe you and Anne are sisters," Lane said as they came to the end of their first block. "You seem as different as night and day."

"Yeah...and Anne would probably be day." She laughed, trying to sound light. "Because she is usually so sunny and bright and positive."

"She's definitely upbeat."

"Whereas I tend to be the realist...or as my mom says the pessimist."

"Like the Valentine Grinch?" he teased.

"Exactly." Her feet started to slide and he steadied her.

"Easy does it."

"Thanks." She sighed, trying to relax and wishing he hadn't brought up Anne. But then maybe it was for the best. And since he had, she decided to take it to the next level. "So do you know Gerard...Anne's ex?"

"Yeah. He was one of the first people I met in town. He was coaching Tristan's soccer team and doing a great job of it."

"So you guys were friends then?" Her tone was cautious.

"Sure. Gerard is a good guy."

"I thought so too. I'm still trying to wrap my head around what went wrong with them."

Lane tightened his grip on her hand as they stepped from the curb to cross the street. "Be careful, I think this is going to be trickier than the sidewalk."

After a couple of close calls, they made it across. "Whew." Emma let out a slow breath. "This is not easy."

"Maybe we should sing," Lane suggested.

"Sing?"

"Sure." And now he launched into the old Dean Martin song "That's Amore." "When the moon hits your eye like a big pizza pie, that's amore. . . ." And now she joined into the lilting tune and was pleasantly surprised to see that the rhythm of the music really did lend itself to skating. "That's amore!"

Before long—and far too soon—they were at Nona's house. Lane guided her along the footpath and safely up the porch steps. "Thank you so much," she told him happily. "That was actually pretty fun."

"It was an enjoyable skate," he said as he released her hand, holding on to the railing as he carefully slid down the steps then turned around. "Thank you for being my partner." He made an awkward bow that narrowly missed becoming another fall, but fortunately he caught his balance before going down.

"You be careful," she warned.

"Will do," he promised as he slowly turned around. "And you get in the house and get warm, Emma."

"I think I'll stay right here and make sure you make it safely home," she called out. "I'd hate to find you frozen to the sidewalk with a broken neck in the morning."

He laughed and then broke into another round of "That's Amore" as he continued skating down the street. Not feeling the least bit cold, she watched with amusement until he turned up the walk to the McCormick house. But as she

turned to go into the house, she experienced a confused mixture of sadness and hope.

The next day the sun came out and the ice from the previous
night was just a memory...a very baffling memory. But
Emma tried to put it behind her as she helped Nona with
the household chores during the morning. Finally it was after
lunch and Emma had done all she could to be sure Nona was
cared for and comfortable.

"I wanted to go set up a Valentine's Day book table," she
explained as she set a mug of tea by Nona's chair. "Just like
Poppi used to do."

"Oh, yes, that is good." Nona nodded approvingly. "Do not
worry about me, *dolce*, I am just fine on my own. You and your
mama, you make too much of me. I am not an invalid."

"I'll only be an hour or so," Emma promised.

"An hour or three hours...does not matter." Nona waved
her hand. "I am fine, *cara mia*. I will probably just take a nap
anyway."

"I'll be home in time to fix dinner," Emma assured her.
"Wait for me."

As Emma walked to town, she couldn't believe how little
time it took compared to last night, when it had felt like
an obstacle course—okay, it was a fun obstacle course. It was
funny, the difference a few unexpected elements could make
to a journey.

Entering the bookstore, it was fun to see the colorful
Valentine's Day decorations suspended from the ceilings and
adorning the walls. They really had done a knock-up job last
night.

"Emma," Virginia called out from behind the coffee
counter. "You did a wonderful job on the decorations."

"How did you know I did it?" Emma asked her as she unwound her scarf.

"Lane was down for coffee." The older woman grinned. "He always gets his coffee here."

"Aha." Emma sniffed the coffee-scented air. "And I can understand why. It smells delicious in here."

"What can I get you?"

Emma ordered a latte. "So...did Lane tell you that he helped me with it?"

"I got that impression." Virginia rinsed a cup in hot water.

"I doubt I could've done it without him."

"He's a good guy. Poppi really enjoyed his company."

"So I gather." As Emma unbuttoned her coat, she explained today's mission. "I know how Poppi loved having his Valentine's Day table right up front. And I know you and Cindy are probably busy just running this store. Between the back room and the front register and the coffee bar, well, I thought I could help out a little."

"That's right." Virginia set her latte on the counter. "I completely forgot about the table."

"I would thoroughly enjoy putting it together."

"Bless you, Emma." Virginia pushed a strand of gray hair away from her glasses. "Poppi would be happy to know that Valentine's Day is in such good hands."

As Emma sipped the delicious hot coffee, looking around the cheerful bookstore, she wondered if last night had been the final execution of Emma's Valentine's Day Grinch. Because today she felt happy and upbeat and hopeful. And yet at the same time there was a faint shadow of melancholy over her. But that was probably due to missing Poppi—especially being here in the bookstore in the daylight hours. She expected to see him popping around the corner with an armload of new books to be shelved. Or talking to a customer, trying to convey his love of reading and the classics, promising "you're going to love this or I'll give you your money back." Very few disgruntled customers ever returned books. If they did, they didn't usually come into the store again and that was probably just as well.

Emma perused the shelves, selecting the usual titles that Poppi would pick for the Valentine's Day table. Of course, she would include the Jane Austen books—after all, she and her sister were named after Austen characters. She also picked the Brontë sisters' novels and *The Scarlet Pimpernel, Gone with the Wind*, and *Anna Karenina*, which though romantic ended sadly...not unlike real life sometimes. She selected *Rebecca* and *Middlemarch*, and for younger readers she put out *Anne of Green Gables* and *Little Women*. Besides prettily arranging the books on a red table cloth and white paper doilies, she also set out some boxes of chocolates and book accessories that looked festive, and by the time she was done, both Cindy and Virginia came over to praise her work.

"That looks beautiful," Cindy told her.

"Poppi would be proud," Virginia proclaimed.

"Thanks," Emma said. "That was fun. If you don't mind, I'll do another little table over by the coffee lounge."

"Oh, that's a good idea," Virginia said. "I even have some mugs you might want to put out."

Emma was just starting on the coffee lounge table when Tristan came wandering in. With his stocking cap sitting lopsided on his head and his backpack dragging behind him on the floor, he looked a bit bedraggled and weary. Not to mention slightly lost.

"Tristan!" Emma happily went over to hug him. "How *are* you?"

He shrugged. "Okay."

"You look tired. Hard day?"

He shrugged again then sniffed loudly.

She reached for a napkin and handed it to him. "For your nose," she said quietly.

He wiped it then stuffed it into his coat pocket.

"Need a cocoa to warm you up?" she asked.

Now he smiled, nodding eagerly.

"Go put your stuff away," she said. "I'll order your cocoa. Whipped cream?"

"Yeah," he called as he hurried over to a table by the window.

She ordered the cocoa then returned to where Tristan was dropping his backpack on the floor by the table. "Mom's gotta work at the gallery late tonight," he told her as he peeled off his coat. "She told me to come over here." He glanced around with a sad expression, as if looking for someone. "But Poppi's not here anymore," he said quietly. "It feels kinda weird."

"Oh…yeah…" Emma nodded. "Did you used to spend time with Poppi after school?"

"Uh-huh." Tristan pulled off his hat, leaving his dark hair sticking out like a scarecrow's. "Mr. Steiner—that's the guy who owns the gallery—he don't like having kids around. He's always saying I'll break something. But I never did. So Mom always tells me to go find Poppi." He wiped his nose on his sleeve. "But Poppi's gone."

"Well, I'm here now." Emma smiled and ruffled his messy hair. "Do you mind spending time with me?"

His brown eyes lit up. "No. What're you doing, Aunt Emma?"

She pointed out the decorations. "I got the Valentine's decorations up last night and today I'm getting the tables set up. Want to help?"

And so, after he finished his cocoa and used the bathroom and washed his hands, Emma put him to work cutting out hearts to decorate the table. By folding the red and pink construction paper like an accordion, they made chains of connected hearts, using them as a border going all around the table. It looked so pretty that they continued making these chains for the coffee counter as well. When they were done, everyone agreed that it was beautiful—and that Poppi would be delighted.

# Chapter 7

By four thirty Emma felt it was time to get back to check on Nona. "Do you think your mom will mind if I take you home with me? I mean to Nona's?"

"She won't care."

"But we should let her know, right?"

Tristan produced a cell phone from his backpack.

"You have your own cell phone?" She blinked. "Impressive."

He grinned. "Yeah. But it's only to call Mom. Or emergencies."

Soon it was settled that he could go with Emma and they were on their way. As she drove, he confessed to her that he missed his dad.

"When will you get to see him again?" she asked.

"Not until spring break. Mom said I get to fly on a plane to go see him." Tristan brightened. "Dad is gonna take me to Disney World."

"Wow. That sounds like fun."

"Uh-huh. I guess so."

"You *guess* so?" She glanced at him as she pulled into the driveway.

"I just wish Mom would come too."

"Oh..."

"Dad even said he'd buy her a plane ticket if she would come."

"Really?"

"Yeah. But she said no. She has to work."

"Well...anyway..." She turned off her car. "You're going to Disney World, Tristan. That is so cool. I've never been there. You'll have to tell me all about it when you get back."

"Will you still be here then?" he asked as they got out. "Or are you going back to Seattle?"

"I think I'll be here. I don't really have any plans to return to Seattle."

He nodded as he hoisted up his backpack. "That's good."

Nona was pleased to see Tristan and even played checkers with him while Emma started dinner. Then Tristan helped by setting the table, and by the time everything was ready, Saundra was getting home.

"Well, we're just one big happy family, aren't we?" she said as she hugged Tristan.

"Four generations all at one table," Nona proclaimed. "That is good luck."

"Good luck?" Tristan asked. "What will happen?"

"We will enjoy each other's company," Nona told him.

And they did. After dinner, Tristan worked on his homework as Emma washed dishes. But finally it was close to eight and Emma was concerned about his bedtime. "Why don't you call your mom and see what she wants you to do?" Emma told him as she turned the lights off in the kitchen. Nona had gone to bed and Saundra was watching some home renovation show on the small TV in the living room. "Maybe you can just spend the night here."

"Really?" he asked with enthusiasm. "On a school night?"

"Well, if she's not home."

Tristan called on his phone and talked for a bit then handed it over to Emma. "She wants to talk to you."

"Hey, Emma," Anne said, "that's sweet you offered to let him spend the night, but I should be done here within the hour. Any chance you can drop him home and I'll be along as soon as I'm finished? That way Trist can get to bed."

"Sure I can do that. But I don't have a key."

"Tristan has a key."

"Okay. I'll see you there then." Emma hung up and explained to her mom and soon they were on their way. Emma hadn't been to Anne's condo in a couple of years, but she knew where it was. And Tristan, pretending like she didn't, directed her all the way there. Then, acting like the man of the house, he unlocked the door and let her inside.

"You should probably start getting ready for bed," she told him. "I promised your mom you would."

"Okay." He tossed his backpack and things on the floor and headed off to his room.

Emma looked around the condo. Her mom hadn't been kidding. Anne had completely redone the place. And it looked like she'd spared no expense either. The eighties-style kitchen cabinets had all been replaced with sleek dark wood. The countertops were granite and the appliances were stainless. Very uptown. But it seemed odd since Emma remembered how the last time she was here, both Anne and Gerard had been talking about selling their condo and getting a real house so that Tristan would have a yard. Apparently they'd changed their minds about that. Or maybe they thought the remodel would help to sell the unit. Anyway, it wasn't Emma's business.

She continued checking out the upgrades, admiring the sleek modern furnishings, the art on the wall, and a gorgeous bouquet of red roses on the dining room table. She did a quick count on the blooms to discover it was not just one dozen, but two. Someone was a big spender. Was it Lane? And if so, what did it mean? That he was just as serious about Anne as she appeared to be about him?

Just then Tristan came bounding in, wearing his pajamas and announcing he'd brushed his teeth and asking if he could play video games.

"I don't think so," she told him in what she hoped was a firm tone. "According to your mom, it's already well past your bedtime." She followed him into his room, noticing the stack of books by his bed. They'd probably been given to him by Poppi. "And you're probably too old for someone to read to you before bed." She reached for the light by his bed.

"No, I'm not," he told her. "Poppi used to read to me when I spent the night over there. I liked it."

"Oh...?" Emma picked up two books from the top of the pile. "*Tom Sawyer* or *The Hobbit*?"

"*The Hobbit*," he said eagerly. "I haven't even started that one yet."

And so she opened *The Hobbit* and started to read. She was just finishing the first chapter when she heard Anne coming into the house. "Goodnight, Tristan," she said quietly, realizing that he was already half asleep. "Sweet dreams." She clicked off the light and tiptoed from the room.

"Oh, there you are," Anne said as she removed an elegant-looking long coat and a pale blue silky scarf. She kicked off her heels and stretched her arms up. "I'm exhausted."

"Long day, eh?" Emma couldn't believe how fresh and perfect Anne looked, especially after working in the gallery all day and half of the night. How did she do it?

"Oh, yeah." Anne went to fridge and removed a bottle of water, opening it and taking a long sip. "You want one?"

"No thanks." Emma moved toward the door. "I should be going."

"So soon?" Anne turned and smiled. "We've hardly spent any time together, Em. Can't you stay awhile?"

Emma shrugged. "Sure. If you're not too tired."

"Come and sit." Anne went into the living room area, settling down onto the white sectional. "You sure you don't want something to drink? Help yourself, if you do."

"No, I'm fine." Emma walked past the dining room table then paused. "Anne, these roses are gorgeous."

Anne took a long sip of water then sighed. "They are pretty, aren't they?"

Emma bent down to sniff, but they had no smell. "A little early for Valentine's Day . . . who's the admirer?"

Anne gave Emma a sly look now. "Who do you think it is?"

Emma felt her cheeks growing warm. Of course, it had to be Lane. "I don't know, Anne. A pretty girl like you probably has lots of admirers."

Anne laughed. "But only a few that I really care about."

"A few?"

She grinned. "Okay, make that one."

"Lane Forester?"

Anne's face broke into a big smile. "Isn't he wonderful?"

Emma came into the living room area, just standing. "He's a very nice man, Anne."

"So you approve?"

"Of course. Why wouldn't I?"

Anne shrugged and took another long swig. "I don't know.
I just want everyone in the family to like him."

"We all liked Gerard," Emma said quietly.

Now Anne's smile vanished.

"I'm sorry..." Emma put her hand on the back of a chair.
"I guess I just don't get it. Gerard seemed like a good guy
and—"

"Please, Emma." Anne stood now. "I really don't want to
talk about it."

"Sorry."

"That era of my life is over. End of story." Anne made a stiff
smile. "I understand you don't get it. But it's not for you to
get. You know? So let's just let it go." She stretched and suppressed a yawn. "And now that I think of it, I really am more
tired than I realized. And tomorrow is another big day. You
know the Big Brothers Big Sisters benefit is tomorrow night.
That's why I was so busy today."

"That's right. I promised Lane I'd come to it."

Anne tipped her head to one side as if she was thinking.
"Well, sure, you can come if you want, Em. But I'll forewarn
you, it'll be pretty sedate. Just a bunch of older people with
deep pockets and some wall space to fill, if you know what I
mean. I doubt you'll even know anyone there. And I'm sure
you don't want to buy any of the pieces...I mean since you
don't even have a home to put them in." She smiled. "I'd completely forgive you if you decide not to come." She placed a
manicured finger next to her cheek. "In fact, if you're interested, maybe I could entice you to spend the evening with
Tristan instead."

"Oh...he's not going to the show?"

Anne laughed. "You think I can manage a ten-year-old and an art show at the same time? I think not."

Emma considered this. "Okay, sure, I'd be happy to spend the evening with Tristan. Do you want him to spend the night at Nona's?"

"That would be divine, Emma." Anne came over and hugged her. "Thank you, dear sister."

"No problem." Emma forced a smile.

"Do you mind if he goes to the bookstore again after school?"

"That's fine."

"I sure miss having Poppi there," Anne said sadly. "It was so good knowing that Tristan could spend time with him. He'd do his homework there and read and all kinds of stuff. I know poor Trist is going to miss it too."

Emma nodded. "Yeah...I know."

"So I guess I'll see you...Saturday then?" Anne was removing her pearl earrings. "Maybe not until past noon if you don't mind. I know I'll be exhausted after Friday night."

"Noon is fine. Want me to bring him by here?"

"Oh, no, that's okay. I can pick him up."

Emma just nodded then told her sister goodnight and left. As she walked through the dark parking lot, relieved there was no freezing rain tonight, she couldn't help but feel slightly dismissed...and dismayed...and disturbed. But maybe it's what she deserved. This is what she got for allowing herself to be interested in her sister's beau. She was simply getting her just deserts. The sooner she forgot about the evening with Lane at the bookstore, the better off they all would be.

# Chapter 8

On Friday, Emma stayed with Nona for most of the day. Helping to catch up with some of the more arduous housekeeping chores, things that had been neglected due to Nona's health and age, Emma had decided to attack one room at a time. Today she had chosen to work on the kitchen by deep cleaning the stove area and beneath the fridge and scrubbing and sealing the grout around the tiles on the counter. But by three o'clock, she was on her way to meet Tristan at the bookstore.

Like yesterday, she got him a cocoa and they sat together at the table by the window, discussing his day at school. He seemed to soak up the attention she was giving him, and she suspected it had as much to do with his absent father as his overly busy mother. Also, like her, he was missing Poppi. Really, they were good company for each other.

They were just finishing up their cocoas when Lane came into the bookstore. Spotting the two of them, he waved enthusiastically then came over, greeting them both warmly. "Mind if I join you?" he asked.

"Not at all," Emma told him.

"I get to spend the night with Aunt Emma and Nona tonight," Tristan told him. "We're going to watch movies and eat pizza and stay up late."

"Really?" Lane's brow creased. "But what about the fundraiser? You're not coming to that? We're going to have great food and music and a magician."

"A magician?" Tristan looked impressed. "For real?"

"I thought the kids might like it." Lane chuckled. "And me too."

"Kids will be at the art show?" Emma asked.

"Yeah, I expect some of the Big Brothers Big Sisters kids to show up," Lane said. "That's why I thought a magician would be fun. And he's really good. Marco the Magnificent. I've seen him before and his hands are way quicker than the eye."

"I want to see the magician," Tristan said eagerly. "I got a magic kit for Christmas and I've been practicing some magic tricks."

"Then come," Lane insisted.

"Can we go, Aunt Emma?"

She tried to remember her sister's reasoning for not wanting him there. Wasn't it because she'd have her hands full with the show? "Sure, I don't see why not."

Tristan grinned.

She looked down at his T-shirt, where he was still wearing what appeared to be part of his lunch. "But I suspect this is a dress-up affair." She glanced at Lane. "Right?"

"It's supposed to be a little uptown, but it probably doesn't really matter if—"

"I have my suit—the one I wore to Poppi's funeral,"

Tristan told her. "It's at home, but we can get it, can't we? I have my key. Can we go, *please*?"

"I guess we can...." Emma wondered if she should check with Anne.

"Your suit will be perfect," Lane told Tristan.

"Well, with this change of plans, we should get going," Emma told Tristan. "We have a lot to do before then."

"Will we still get to watch movies and eat pizza and stay up late?" he asked, "I mean after the fundraiser?"

She laughed. "This guy wants his cake and to eat it too."

Tristan looked hopeful. "We're having cake?"

Lane chuckled. "See you two later then."

Emma and Tristan told Lane goodbye then went on their way. Emma couldn't help but feel a bit sneaky as she drove Tristan over to the condo, letting themselves in and helping him pick up his things. But she remembered how Anne had specifically told her this event was boring and better suited for old people—almost as if she didn't want Emma there. Well, what was up with that?

Back at Nona's, Emma kept her promise to Tristan by ordering pizza for dinner for everyone. Not only did this please her nephew but it also gave her a little time to think about what she could wear for the evening. While Tristan visited with Nona, Emma went through the closet where she'd recently hung up her clothes, looking for something "uptown." Her sapphire blue velvet cocktail dress seemed a little over the top for this small town, but she thought she'd be safe anywhere in her little black dress. Elegant but conservative, and with a quick steaming it looked as good as ever. With this she would wear the silver heart-shaped locket Poppi had given her for her sixteenth birthday. Juvenile perhaps, but it always made her feel good to wear it. Combine those with silver hoop earrings and her good black heels and she should be presentable enough for an art show. Plus she would pin her hair up in a loose curly bun. Not nearly as sleek as Anne would be, but it might add a touch of sophistication.

As they were eating pizza, Saundra announced that she wanted to go to the fundraiser as well, suggesting the three of them go together. "What about you, Nona?" Emma asked. "Do you feel like coming?"

"No, no, I do not wish to go. *Grazie.*"

"But will you be all right here by yourself?"

"Yes, yes. I told you already. I am not sick, *dolce.* I do not need to be watched. I will go to bed right after *Jeopardy!* and I will be just fine."

"And we'll be home by eight," Saundra assured her. "I know I won't want to stay more than an hour."

So it was settled. Everyone went off to get ready, with Nona insisting on helping Tristan. When Emma emerged from her room, feeling good in her little black dress and just putting on her trench coat, she was met by her frowning mother.

"*What?*" Saundra pointed at her. "Is that the only coat you have?"

"What's wrong with it?"

"Nothing if you're waiting for a bus in a rainstorm."

"Huh?" Emma looked down at the tan trench coat.

"Wait a minute." Saundra held up a hand. "I have something you can wear."

"*Mom,*" Emma called, following her. "You are three inches shorter than me and—"

"No, no, it'll work," Saundra called over her shoulder as she pawed through the little closet. "You'll see."

Emma stood in the doorway of the sewing room, waiting

as Saundra dug and complained about the size of closets in old homes. "Really, someone should come up with an add-on design that would instantly pop a full-size walk-in into an old home like this. They would become an instant millionaire."

"Are you ready yet?" Tristan yelled from downstairs.

"In a minute," Emma called back.

"Here it is." Saundra emerged holding up a cranberry red mohair coat.

"Mom, that's a beautiful coat, but I can't imagine it's going to fit me."

"Try it on, Emma."

So Emma hung her trench coat on the doorknob and slipped on the red coat. With its rich satiny lining and soft fuzzy exterior, it felt luxurious and warm and truly wonderful. "It's absolutely yummy," Emma admitted. "But does it really work on me?" She gave a spin, causing the full hem of the coat to flare out. And, really, the length wasn't bad either, barely below her knees. Maybe it was okay.

"It's too long for me." Saundra guided Emma over to the freestanding mirror that Nona had kept in the sewing room for as long as Emma could remember. "But, see, Emma, it's perfect on you."

Emma stared in wonder at the magical red coat. "Oh, Mom, it's really gorgeous. I totally love it. Are you sure you want me to wear it? What if I spill something?"

"It's yours, my dear."

"Are you certain—"

"I am positive. It's perfect on you. Nothing about it was right for me," Saundra explained as they went downstairs. "Too long. Too much color. Really it was all wrong for me. Although I'll admit it's a gorgeous garment and I know it was costly."

"Then why did you get it—if it was all wrong?" Emma asked at the foot of the stairs.

"Oh, I didn't get it. Your father did."

"Oh..."

"Look at you," Nona said as she and Tristan came to the foot of the stairs. "Oh, Emma, you look like a queen. *Bellissima!*" Nona clapped her hands and her eyes lit up. "Oh, *dolce,* you are *bellissima!*"

"What about me?" Saundra demanded in a teasing tone.

"Oh, yes, yes," Nona assured her, "you are *bellissima* too."

"And me?" Tristan asked. "Am I *bellissima* too?"

Nona laughed. "No, no. You are *bello.*"

"Because you are a boy," Emma explained.

"We better go, Nona." Saundra jingled her car keys. "And since we all look so beautiful, I am driving my fine carriage tonight. We must travel in style. Now let's get moving, kiddos."

Emma tried not to feel nervous as her mother drove them the few blocks to town. She knew she had every right to attend this public fundraiser, but she also knew that Anne would probably not like it—even though that made no sense.

"Now, Tristan," Emma said as Saundra was parking down the street. "You are kind of like our date tonight, *right, Mom?*"

"That's right."

"So we want you on your best behavior."

"I'll be good," he promised from the backseat.

"And if you're not..." She tried to think of something. "Then we won't be able to watch our movie and stay up late like we wanted to. *Okay?*"

"Okay."

"Because this is your mother's big night at the gallery,"

Saundra said as she turned off the car. "You must be on your best behavior."

"I know, I know." He sounded a little exasperated.

"And for Lane's sake too," Emma pointed out. "Remember this is for Big Brothers Big Sisters. It's to raise funds for the foundation. You should do your part."

"I will," he said more firmly.

As they got out of the car, about a block from the gallery, Emma could see it well lit with festive strings of white lights on the awnings. And along the sidewalk, lines of luminarias led up to the front door. Very pretty and festive and fun. The cheerful sound of music greeted them as they went inside and suddenly Emma was glad that she'd come.

"There's the magician," Tristan whispered to Emma, pointing to a corner where some kids were already gathering around a man in the black tuxedo. "Can I go and watch now?"

"Sure." She patted his back. "Just mind your manners."

He nodded, but his eyes were fixed on the magician. Emma paused to watch as the mysterious man gracefully waved a wand over his black silk hat then pulled out a bunch of bright-colored flowers. The children were mesmerized. Meanwhile Saundra was being greeted by a friend, and now Emma, left to her own devices, decided to simply wander through the gallery. It would be interesting to see the local artists' works. And to her surprise some of them seemed to have real talent. She paused to look at a well-done still life, studying it closely.

"Hello, Miss Burcelli."

Emma turned to see Lane smiling at her. He had on a nicely tailored suit, similar to the one he wore to the funeral, only this one was black. She returned his smile. "Hello, Mr. Forester."

"Last names seem a bit formal, don't they?" He chuckled.

"Especially after our ice escapades the other night. Did you end up with any bruises?"

"As a matter of fact, yes." She giggled. "That was the strangest weather. It almost seems surreal now."

He looked directly into her eyes with an intensity that caused her heart to do a little flip-flop. "Actually it seems rather dreamlike to me. Wine and chocolate and Dean Martin and ice skating. That'll be a hard evening to surpass, don't you think?"

She felt her cheeks warming. What was he really saying? Was he flirting with her? Or was she just delirious? "Well, I must admit I have an earworm I can't seem to eradicate."

"What?" He looked alarmed. "An earworm?"

She laughed. "It means when a song keeps looping through your ear. An earworm."

"Oh." He looked relieved but slightly confused.

"'That's Amore,'" she explained. "I can't seem to get it out of my head."

He laughed. "Oh, yeah, I know exactly what you—"

*"Lane."* Anne swooped up from behind him, slipping her arm into his. "There you—" She stopped mid-sentence, looking slightly stunned to see that it was Emma who was conversing with him.

"Hi, Anne," Emma said meekly.

"Oh, Em! I didn't expect to see *you* here tonight." Her brow creased with concern. "Wait, if you're here... *where is Tristan?*"

"I invited them to come," Lane explained to Anne. "Tristan didn't realize there was a magician tonight and I thought he should—"

"So, Trist is here?" Anne's eyes darted around the increasingly crowded gallery. "But did he get cleaned up after school? I can only imagine—"

"He looks like a perfect gentleman," Emma assured her. "Besides that he's been lectured on how to mind his manners. He's over there watching the magician right now."

"Oh..." Anne still looked disconcerted, but her shell pink lips curled into a stiff smile. "*Lane*," she said in a honey-coated voice, "I was coming to get you. I need you to meet someone really important." She glanced back at Emma. "You will excuse us, won't you?"

"Certainly." Emma gave her sister an uneasy smile.

"Catch you later," Lane called lightly over his shoulder, but he gave her a friendly little wave as Anne swooshed him away. Emma tried not to feel envious of her pretty little sister. After all this was supposed to be Anne's night. Not Emma's. And she looked so chic in her pale pink fitted dress and those dainty matching shoes, with every sleek blonde hair in place. Anne was as pretty as a picture, and she probably knew it. Just the same Emma tried not to compare herself to Anne's delicately perfect appearance. Like Lane had said, they were as different as night and day...and that was okay.

Emma continued to survey the art pieces, but her mind was still stuck on the conversation she'd been having—or almost having—with Lane. Was she imagining it, or was he flirting with her? And if he was flirting with her, should she be alarmed? Or insulted? Or just plain confused? And what about those red roses he'd sent to her sister—

"Emma!" Her father eagerly grasped her by the hand. "I was hoping to see you here tonight." Now he stared at her coat with a slightly puzzled expression. "You look very lovely." He rubbed his chin. "You know, I got your mother a coat very similar to that one...this past Christmas."

She gave him a sheepish look. "I know, Dad. *Exactly* like this one."

His brows arched. "Ahhh...I see."

"Mom said it was too big for her...and the wrong color." She smiled happily. "But I adore it. She made me wear it and I must admit that it feels delicious. You have wonderful taste, Daddy."

He laughed. "Well, then it must've been meant for you." He shook his head. "Come to think of it, it doesn't look like your mother's style at all. It belongs on a tall beautiful Italian woman—just like you."

She held her head higher. "Thanks, Dad."

Now they strolled along together, studying and commenting on the various pieces of art. And it was truly enjoyable being with her dad like this. She was surprised that his knowledge of art was more polished than she expected. But it did bother her that her parents couldn't enjoy an evening like this together. That seemed just wrong...and sad.

"Dad?" she began quietly. "Do you even miss Mom?"

He made an attempt at a smile. "Sure, I do. But to be honest, it's been nice and quiet around the house too. Gives a man a chance to reflect."

"And have you been reflecting?"

He nodded. "Some."

"And you're not getting lonely?"

He nodded again. "Some."

"I'm curious, Dad," she lowered her voice, "what would it take to get you two back together?"

He shrugged. "She's the one who left, Emma. She can come back whenever she likes. I haven't changed the locks."

"But maybe you need to *invite* her to come back. Make her feel wanted and loved and appreciated."

"How about me? What if I want to feel wanted and loved and appreciated?"

Another couple was moving closer to them now so Emma just nodded. "I get that," she said evenly. "I just wish you guys could sit down and talk about it."

"I'm perfectly willing."

"So maybe I should be working on, uh, the other party?" she spoke even more guardedly since the room was getting crowded.

He shrugged. "The other party may have already moved on."

"And that's okay with you?"

Rob gave her his business smile although his eyes looked troubled as he waved at some friends of his that were approaching. This conversation was definitely over. And, really, this wasn't the time or place for it anyway. Instead Emma put on her game face too, smiling as her father introduced her to his friends. Then, as they all chatted and commented on the various works of art, she tried to appear involved, but the truth was she was keeping an eye on Lane and Anne. And from what she could see, Anne was keeping Lane on a very short leash tonight.

After a bit, she excused herself to go and check on Tristan and the magic show, but Tristan appeared to be keeping his word and minding his manners. So she just waved at him, then went to see what was displayed in the back section of the gallery. It was quieter back there, and as she perused the paintings, a particular one caught her attention. She wasn't sure what it was that captivated her, because she knew enough about art to know that it wouldn't be considered a great work by anyone. Some might even call it trite or clichéd or overly sweet. But she wouldn't. Plus she knew that the true value of art was always in the eyes of the beholder. And she really liked this piece.

She stepped back to view it better. Simple and straight-forward, it was merely a lighthouse on a craggy piece of shore, shrouded with a dusky fog. But something about the warm glow of the light in the tower and the crashing of the frothy waves below gave her a feeling of safety and shelter and peace. She peered down at the signature to see the name Randolph Lawrence, and although she knew it was a local artist, it didn't ring any bells. She didn't see any other works by this particular painter. But what did it matter? Besides, she reminded herself, this was all for a good cause. And so she removed the card with the price and the item number and took it up to the woman acting as cashier. She paid for her purchase, writing down her name and information on the back of the card.

"You can pick up your painting anytime next week," the woman explained. "We plan to run the exhibit throughout the weekend as well so that any purchases made throughout Sunday will go to the Big Brothers Big Sisters program."

"That's a good idea." Emma slid her debit card back into her purse. "I'll pick it up on Monday. Thanks!"

After a bit Emma found her mother, and they both decided they'd seen enough and were ready to go home. And since the magic show had just ended, Tristan was happy to leave as well. Emma felt slightly bad not to get a chance to speak to Lane again, but it was clear that Anne was not letting him out of her sight. And, after all, he needed to be on hand to speak to the guests about the Big Brothers Big Sisters program.

"Well, that was a nice event," Saundra said they walked to the car. "It looks like they're making some good money too."

"I even bought a painting," Emma told her.

"Really? Which one?"

Emma described the foggy seascape and her mother just

chuckled as they got into the car. "Well, that's very sweet, dear, but I hope you didn't think it was an investment piece."

Emma stifled her irritation as she buckled her seatbelt. "I bought it simply because I *like* it. I plan to hang it in my bedroom, not sell it on Craigslist."

"Yes, and that's perfectly fine. I bought several pieces myself. And I don't expect to get rich from them either. Although I will tack my usual percentage onto them when I use them for some of my clients' homes. But they really will make a nice statement in a couple of projects I'm working on. And it is all for a good cause."

"I talked to Dad for a while," Emma said carefully. She knew this conversation would be limited because of Tristan's ears. But perhaps that would be good—no one could say too much. "He admitted that he misses you."

"Really?"

"I think he wants to talk."

"Really?" she said again.

"Grandma, why are you staying at Nona's house?" Tristan inquired.

"Oh...I thought it would be fun for a while," Saundra said lightly. "To be with Nona and your Aunt Emma...and you tonight. Don't you think that's fun?"

"Yeah!" he said with enthusiasm.

Not for the first time since coming home, Emma felt like she was witnessing the slow but certain unraveling of the Burcelli family. A family that had once been admired greatly by the people in this town, and perhaps those who were unaware still did. Not that Emma cared particularly. But for her parents' sake, and even for poor Tristan, who was humming to himself in the backseat, she did wish her parents would try to work this thing out.

# Chapter 9

On Saturday morning, Anne called at ten and asked Emma if she could get Tristan over to the bookstore by eleven. "I totally forgot it's his Big Brother day," she said sleepily.

"No problem," Emma told her. "He'll be there."

Though she knew he could probably walk to town by himself, especially since it was such a nice sunny day, she still insisted on going with him. After all, she knew this would be her chance to see Lane again. And even if it was only for a few seconds, she was eager to see him. She knew it was juvenile, and she would be embarrassed if anyone suspected her true reasons for walking Tristan the few blocks to town, but she did it just the same.

Lane was just ordering a coffee when they went inside. "Can I get you guys something?" he offered. Tristan said he'd like a cocoa and Emma let him order her latte. But when he handed her coffee to her, she felt uncomfortable. "Thanks," she told him. "But I should go so that you guys get on with your day. I know this is Tristan's special time with you, Lane."

"Yeah, but we're just going to sit here and drink our drinks," he said easily.

"Yeah, Aunt Emma," Tristan told her. "You can stay and drink your coffee."

Still feeling like an intruder, she sat down.

"So what'd you think of the magic show?" Lane asked Tristan.

"It was great. I learned how to do a card trick."

"Cool," Lane told him. "You'll have to show me sometime."

"I wish I had a deck of cards." Tristan frowned.

"They probably sell cards here." Lane pulled out his billfold and handed Tristan a ten. "Go ahead and get some. Then you can show us."

"Thanks!" Tristan leaped to his feet. "I'll be right back."

"That was nice of you," Emma told Lane.

"Or selfish." Lane said, winking mysteriously.

"What?"

"Sorry. I just wanted to have you to myself for a few minutes, Emma. Do you mind?"

"No, no . . . not at all." She gave him puzzled look. "Is, uh, something wrong?"

"No, nothing's wrong. But I had hoped to talk to you more last night and the next thing I knew you were gone. I looked all over and finally asked your dad and he said he'd seen you guys leaving."

She felt her heart fluttering again. Why was he so interested in her whereabouts? "Well, the magic show ended, it was getting late, and my mom wanted to go home."

He nodded. "Yeah. I understand. But I never had a chance

to tell you how beautiful you looked last night." He smiled warmly. "Our conversation was cut short."

"I know. But Anne needed you...and, after all, it was your big night." She felt nervous but slightly delirious. Had he really missed her? But now she didn't know what to say—especially with him gazing at her like that. It was all so unexpected. "So how did it go?" she asked suddenly. "I mean the fundraiser part."

"I haven't heard any numbers, but a fair amount of art was purchased. I know that much. And we still have today and tomorrow to make some sales."

"There was some really nice art there," she said. "I even bought a piece."

"Good for you."

She spotted Tristan hurrying their way with a pack of cards in hand. He opened the cards and explained how the trick was supposed to work. Of course, it took several attempts and some editing help from her and Lane, but eventually Tristan seemed to have it down. "Now I can show my friends at school," he proclaimed happily.

Emma looked at her empty coffee cup then smiled at Lane. "Thanks for the coffee," she told him. "But now I'm going to let you guys get on with your day." She stood. "Have fun!" Then, feeling a broad mixture of emotions, she left. As she walked through town, she felt excited, then worried, then thrilled, and then anxious. But by the time Nona's house came into sight, she felt just plain confused. What was Lane trying to do? He was obviously involved with Anne...and yet he clearly seemed to be flirting with her. What was up with that?

Just as she got near the house, she noticed her dad's car pulling up in front. She looked his direction, giving him a friendly wave, but she could tell by the perplexed look on his face that he didn't even see her. Finally, she went over to the driver's side window to get his attention.

He let the window down with an uneasy expression. "Hey, Emma."

"What'cha up to, Dad? Coming to see Mom?"

"I actually came to see my mom," he confessed. "I usually stop by on Saturday morning. But with your mom's car here...well, I'm not sure what to do. For some reason I thought she'd be gone. She sometimes works on Saturday."

"Maybe she walked to town," Emma suggested. "It's such a nice day."

"Maybe..." He frowned up at the house. "I guess I could call Nona's number. But I hate to disturb her. The phone's in the kitchen, you know, and she could be anywhere."

"Want me to go in ahead of you?" Emma offered. "Make sure the coast is clear?"

He brightened. "Would you, honey?"

"Sure."

Emma went inside to see that Nona was sitting in her chair doing a crossword puzzle. Nona always told everyone that crossword puzzles had helped her English nearly as much as soap operas used to—back before they all turned sleazy.

"Hey, Nona," Emma said. "Is Mom around?"

"I think she's upstairs."

"Okay." Emma glanced to the front door. "Dad wanted to come in and see you, but—"

"Your father's out there?"

"Yes. Want me to tell him to come in?"

"Certainly! Why would he not?"

Emma grimaced. "Because of Mom," she said quietly.

"*Mama mia!*" Nona shook her head. "Such nonsense."

Emma laughed. "I know. I'll tell Dad to come in and then I'll go give Mom a warning."

*"Grazie, cara mia."* Nona set her book and pencil aside. "I'll go put on the teakettle."

Emma went out to wave at her dad, motioning for him to come inside then she hurried upstairs to let her mom know.

"He's here? Now?" Saundra frowned as she pulled a short boot onto her foot. "To see me?"

Emma shrugged. "I think he wants to visit Nona. But maybe it's a multipurpose visit. Who knows?"

"Hmph." Saundra reached for the other boot. "Well, I won't be holding my breath."

"Are you going to work today?"

Saundra shrugged. "I wasn't sure. I have a lunch date at one. Hardly seems worth it to go in for just an hour."

"Do you have a minute to talk?" Emma asked, unsure if this was even a good idea, although she wanted to talk to someone.

"Sure, honey. Is something wrong?"

Emma sat down on the chair by the window. "Maybe."

"What is it?"

"I'm not really sure how to begin," Emma said carefully. "It has to do with Lane Forester."

Saundra's finely plucked brows lifted. "Uh-oh..."

"What do you mean, *uh-oh*?"

"Unless I'm mistaken, you are interested in your sister's boyfriend."

"Is he her boyfriend?" Emma asked.

"You know what I've told you. They're not officially a couple. But you've seen them together, Emma. There's definitely *something* going on there. Don't you think?"

Emma shrugged. "I'm not sure what to think." And now

she told her mother about some of her encounters with Lane. "I'm not saying that he's coming on to me, Mom, but he is being awfully friendly."

"That's because you're Anne's *sister*, Emma. Lane is very friendly to everyone in Anne's family. He has been for some time now." Saundra reached over and patted Emma's hand. "I can understand how you might misinterpret his friendliness as flirting, but I suspect that it's completely innocent. He's just that kind of guy." She smiled dreamily. "Charming and charismatic and warm." She laughed. "Poppi used to tease Lane, saying that he was certain that he was really Italian."

Emma pressed her lips together. "Yeah," she said slowly. "That's probably it, Mom."

"Of course, it is. Lane is looking forward to being part of this family—I just know it!" Saundra clasped her hands together with sparkling eyes. "And I would love to start planning a big beautiful wedding for Anne right now. Not like that poor little excuse of a ceremony she had with Gerard. Good grief, that was a sad little affair. But can you imagine how beautiful I could make everything for them? Maybe a June wedding if we got right on it. We could have the reception at our house. That would give us time to get the yard completely redone. Oh, it would be delightful."

Emma tried to hide her disappointment, but knew her mother was probably right. Besides, she saw an opportunity here. "But if you're going to have the reception at your house, wouldn't it be wise to patch things up with Dad?"

Saundra looked as if her bubble had just been popped. "Well, uh, yes...I suppose so. But there's plenty of time to do that."

"I don't know...June's not that far off, Mom." Emma counted on her fingers. "That's only four or five months away."

Saundra frowned. "Well, maybe a fall wedding would be better."

"Maybe..." Emma stood. "But it might be nice if the happy couple got engaged first...don't you think?"

"Absolutely. In fact, I think I will see if I can drop Lane some hints. Wouldn't it be romantic if they got engaged on Valentine's Day?"

"That would be romantic," Emma said stiffly.

"And we could throw them an engagement party." Saundra stood too, gazing out the window with a wistful expression. "Although I'd have to patch things up with your father...if I wanted to have the party at our house. And that would really be the best place for it, don't you think?"

"Uh-huh." Emma moved to the door. "You better start thinking of what you need to do to mend your fences with Dad, Mom."

Saundra looked hopefully at Emma. "What do you think I should do?"

Emma shrugged. "I'm not exactly an expert in the romance, love, and marriage arena."

"I know, but you're sensible, Emma. What should I do?" Saundra was wringing her hands now.

"Maybe you should learn to cook spaghetti and meatballs," Emma said lightly.

"Spaghetti and meatballs?" Saundra frowned.

"Yeah, for Dad."

"As it so happens, I *can* cook spaghetti and meatballs," Saundra retorted. "Open a jar and open a box, throw it together. Voilà!"

"I mean *homemade* spaghetti sauce. *Homemade* meatballs," Emma clarified. "Even homemade pasta if you want to do it like Nona does. Dad adores her spaghetti and meatballs. And, really, it's not that hard to make. I can even do it, although I usually use packaged pasta."

Saundra blinked. "You can cook?"

"Sure. Nona taught Anne and me when we were kids."

"Anne doesn't cook."

"Well, I wouldn't know about that. But if you wanted to get Dad's attention, it would probably impress him if you cooked him a nice dinner of real spaghetti and meatballs," Emma declared as she went out the door. "And I know that Nona would teach you, if you wanted."

"But why should I cook a special dinner for him?" Saundra demanded. "He's the one who hurt me. He should cook for me."

Emma shrugged. "Maybe so. But you're the one who was planning engagement dinners and weddings and whatnot. I was just trying to help, Mom. You asked."

Saundra nodded with a thoughtful expression. "Yes . . . you may be right."

With so many people under Nona's roof, Emma decided to return to the bookstore and see if she could lend a hand today. She knew that normally Poppi would have been there and, besides that, she was curious to see how the Valentine's tables were doing. Perhaps they needed some attention. Mostly she just wanted to get out of the house.

Virginia and Cindy were both glad to see her. "Saturday is our busy day," Cindy explained as she was teaching Emma how to use the register. "And even more so before a holiday. Next Saturday is just a couple days before Valentine's Day and I expect we'll be really busy."

"Well, I'll make sure to be here for the whole day," Emma promised. "And I don't know why I can't come in every day in the afternoon. Would that help?"

"That'd be fabulous," Cindy told her. "And we got some boxes of books in the back that haven't been shelved yet."

"Want me to start on those?"

"Would you mind?"

"Not at all."

So it was that Emma spent the next couple of hours unpacking books and placing them on the proper shelves. Sure, it wasn't exciting work, but it was fulfilling in its own way. Besides getting to see the new titles, she felt like she was creating order, and that felt good. Maybe it was because so many other parts of her life felt slightly chaotic for the time being. But right here and right now, as she slid the children's picture books onto the big face-out shelf, she felt like she had control of something . . . and it was working for her.

"Hey, Aunt Emma." Tristan tugged on her sleeve, looking up at her with a slightly grubby-looking face. "What'cha doing?"

"Putting books away." She pointed at his chin, which seemed to have the traces of chocolate on it. "Someone needs to check his face," she teased. Now she noticed his hands. "And what would Poppi say about handling books with those?"

He gave her a guilty look as he tucked his hands behind his back. "Oops."

"'Oops' is right. But what are you doing here? I thought this was your Big Brother day. Are you done now?"

"Nope. We did the climbing wall at the sports center and then we had lunch and ice cream. But then I remembered I needed a book on spiders for school. I'm s'posed to write a report. And the library was already closed when we got there. So Lane said I could get a book here."

"Uh-huh." She nodded as she shelved a Curious George book. "And those hands?"

"I'll go wash 'em right now."

She smiled. "And you might be glad to know I just put some bug books out. They looked good too."

As Tristan took off for the restroom, Lane came sauntering over to the children's section. Now, unlike this morning, she didn't feel the least bit eager to see him. What if her mom was right? What if he was simply being charming and wonderful because she was going to be his sister-in-law? How foolish would she feel when she was standing by Anne at their wedding knowing that she'd been over the moon for her sister's groom?

"Hello, Emma," he said warmly. "Helping out?"

She nodded as she slipped another book into place. "Yes, with Poppi gone, I know they're shorthanded." She gave him her professional smile. "And I don't mind. I've always loved being around books."

"But you worked in advertising?"

"Yeah..." She reached for another stack of books. "I discovered I was a pretty good copywriter in college... for some reason that made me think I'd enjoy working in marketing."

"But you didn't?"

"Not so much." She turned over the book in her hand, pointing to the back cover copy and skimming it. "See, I think I could've done this a little better." She pointed to a line. "That doesn't really make sense, does it?"

He studied the line. "Not really."

"But writing sales copy or book cover copy... well, it's not as fulfilling as I'd hoped it would be."

"So what would be your dream job?" he asked as he straightened a crooked book. "Working in a bookstore?"

She shook her head. "No, I don't think that would be my dream job. But it might have something to do with a bookstore."

"Aha..." He nodded with a knowing look. "Then I think I have guessed your dream job."

"What?" She turned and frowned at him. "How is that possible?" She'd never told anyone what her dream job truly was...she barely admitted it to herself...it sounded too foolish and unachievable. How could he know?

"You want to be an author and write books," he stated.

She took in a long slow breath and turned back to the bookshelf. *How did he know?*

"I'm right, aren't I?"

She just shrugged, slowly shelving the books and trying not to act dumbfounded. But how *did* he know?

He chuckled. "I can see it in your eyes, Emma."

"What?"

"Poppi mentioned to me that you used to create books as a little girl. He described how you would write the stories and illustrate them, even binding them together with cardboard covers. I think he might even have some of them stashed away somewhere."

"Oh..." She was partly embarrassed and partly touched.

"And why shouldn't you be an author?" he persisted.

She gave him her are-you-crazy look. "Because it's impossible!"

He waved his hand toward the stacks of shelves. "What if all these people, the ones who wrote these books, thought that?"

She frowned. "But look at all these books, Lane, and this is just a small portion of what's out there. Why does anyone even need to write another?"

He laughed. "I'm sure glad that the other authors out there don't think like that. Imagine all the wonderful stories that we'd miss out on."

She grimaced. What he said actually made sense, but she didn't want to admit it. And seeing Tristan coming this way, she knew she wouldn't have to. "Excuse me," she told him. "I want to show Tristan the new bug books that just came in. I think he'll like them."

As she was showing Tristan the science section and the new books, she knew that Lane was watching them. And that only served to aggravate her more. Did he really think it was okay to play the charmer, to toy with someone's heart like this—just because he wanted to endear himself to Anne's family? Didn't he realize the havoc he could create if he wanted to? Didn't he care?

# Chapter 10

On Sunday, Emma went to church with Nona and her mother, but because Nona was moving slowly, they arrived a few minutes late. However, Nona's favorite pew had enough space for them to squeeze in. Sitting directly ahead of them were Anne and Tristan and Lane—like the perfect little family. Tristan was sitting in the middle, but after Reverend Thomas announced it was time for children's church, Anne scooted over so that she was sitting right next to Lane—like the perfect couple. And certainly they looked perfect together. There probably weren't two more attractive people in the church. Emma tried to focus on the sermon, but all she could think about was Anne and Lane. Why didn't they just proclaim themselves a couple, get engaged, and start planning their wedding? It would certainly make her mother happy.

Sitting on the other side of the aisle was Emma's dad. With his eyes straight forward, it almost seemed like he was paying attention. And that was reassuring. It was also reassuring to see him here. She remembered a time when her mother had to nag and pester her dad to go to church. With her being gone, it would've been easy for him to have slept in and pretend to forget it was Sunday. Yet, here he was. It gave Emma hope.

After the service, Lane and Anne turned around and started visiting with them just as easily and naturally as anything. But all Emma wanted to do was run.

"I'm glad to see you," Lane told her. "I want to ask you a favor."

"A favor?"

"Yes. Will you have coffee with me tomorrow morning?"

Emma felt her cheeks warming. She could tell that Saundra and Anne and Nona were all curiously watching her. "Tomorrow morning?" she echoed meekly. "I . . . uh . . . have to help with Nona and—"

"Nonsense," Nona told her. "I am fine, Emma. You go and have coffee."

"But I like to help you with—"

"You baby me too much," Nona insisted. "You will turn me into an invalid, *dolce*. Go and have coffee with Lane."

"But I—"

"I could come to your house for coffee," Lane offered. "Is ten okay?"

She nodded. "Sure. That would work."

"Good." He smiled. "I need some help with my ad campaign for KidsPlay. And maybe we can talk about Big Brothers Big Sisters while we're at it."

"Oh," Anne said with what seemed like relief. "This is work for you, Emma. How nice."

Lane tossed Anne a curious look. "Well, hopefully it's more than just work. I consider Emma my friend too."

Anne gave him a sugary smile. "I certainly hope so, Lane. She is my only sister."

Emma felt like running now. This was all too weird, too uncomfortable. Seeing her dad near the door, she used him as her excuse. "I'm sorry," she told them. "I need to go speak to Dad about something." She hurried over to him and asked if they could have coffee together.

"You bet." He nodded. "I'd like that."

"Can I ride with you?" she asked helplessly.

"Sure." He peered curiously at her. "Something wrong?"

"Maybe." She nudged him toward the door. "Let's get out of here, okay?"

As they walked to his car, she told him that she was confused and flustered and in need of some fatherly advice.

"About what?" he asked as they got into his Saab.

And so, similar to what she'd told her mom, she poured out her story about Lane to him. "And Mom says Lane is just friendly like that to everyone. But I keep getting a feeling that it's something more—like he's really interested in me. But I know that makes no sense. Do you think I'm crazy?"

"Not in the least."

Before long they were seated at Starbucks, because Emma was worried that she might see Lane at the bookstore, although he probably didn't go to his office on Sunday. "I don't know what to do, Dad. It's not like I'm trying to initiate anything with him. I know that Anne is really into him."

"But is he into her?" her dad asked.

"It's weird...Lane treats her politely, but he's kind of cool to her too. Have you noticed that?"

"I've noticed that Anne seems to be trying too hard to get him." He gave his coffee a stir. "The way she chases after him, dragging him around like she owns him. I even told her that she might be blowing it. Some guys like to be the hunters, you know. She might get further by playing hard to get."

"Really, you think that she's trying too hard?"

He nodded and took a sip.

"And that Lane might not be as into her as she thinks?" Emma felt a small rush of hope. "But Anne is so pretty, Dad. She could probably get any man she liked."

Her dad's brow creased. "Do you think Anne is prettier than you?"

Emma gave him a look that said *duh*.

Now her dad peered curiously at her. "Emma, you are a beautiful woman. Don't you know that?"

She smiled at him. "Thanks, Dad. But you're my dad; you're supposed to think that."

He rolled his eyes. "And as you well know, I'm no expert in the area of romance. Your mother has made that absolutely clear to me over the years. So much so that I just gave up even trying."

"You gave up on romance?" Emma felt sad to hear this.

He just nodded.

"Do you still love Mom?"

Her dad looked down at his coffee.

"Is there someone else?" she asked in a tiny voice.

He looked up with alarm. "No, no, certainly not."

She sighed, believing him. "But you didn't answer me...do you still love Mom?"

"Of course, I do." He frowned. "Just don't tell her I said that."

"You two." She shook her head. "You're being so childish."

"Unlike you and your sister and the man you both want?"

She frowned. "I never said I *wanted* him, Dad."

"Not in so many words..."

"It's just that I'm confused. I don't know what to do."

"You know what Poppi would tell you to do, don't you?"

"What's that?" She studied him.

"Follow your heart."

"Oh...yeah..."

"We're a pair, aren't we? Sitting here and trying to figure out our love lives when it's obvious we're both in the dark and yet we're trying to give each other advice." He laughed. "Like the blind leading the blind."

She pointed her finger at him. "Want some advice...from your blind daughter?"

He smiled. "Sure."

"You love spaghetti and meatballs, right?"

He nodded. "You know I do."

"And it bugs you that Mom doesn't know how to make it?"

He shrugged. "I don't know...maybe...a little. But that's not really it, Emma."

"I know. But how about this—how about if you learn to make it and you make it for Mom? It could be a peace-making meal."

He seemed to be thinking about this.

"It's really easy, Dad. Nona or I could teach you. And we both know that Mom is never going to be much of a cook. But you always seemed to like the kitchen."

He smiled. "I think I'd be a good cook."

"So why not let us teach you a few tricks. It'd be fun."

"All right." He nodded. "How do we go about this?"

And so they started putting together a plan for how he would come over to Nona's for an afternoon or two next week and learn to cook.

"At the very least I won't have to live off of takeout every night," he said.

"And Nona will love teaching you."

On Monday morning, Emma felt nervous and torn. She wanted to see Lane...and yet she didn't. Finally, as she was finishing up the breakfast dishes she reminded herself, *This is business—purely business.* Lane needed advertising help. She would give it to him. End of story.

Lane arrived at ten o'clock on the dot. And he looked sharp in his khaki slacks and dark brown polo sweater. As she opened the front door, she instantly wished she'd put on something nicer than her favorite jeans and black turtleneck. But then she reminded herself again, *This is business—purely business.* Her appearance was of no consequence.

"Good morning, Mrs. Burcelli," he told Nona as they passed through the living room.

"Why do you not call me Nona?" she asked. "You called my husband Poppi; you should call me Nona. No?"

He grinned. "All right, I will. Thank you, *Nona.*"

"That's better." She grinned at him then turned her attention back to her knitting.

"Coffee is in the kitchen," Emma said in a businesslike tone. "I figured we could work in there, if you don't mind."

"Sounds good to me." He followed her into the kitchen, waiting as she poured him a cup of coffee, showing him the cream and sugar on the counter. "I've only been in this kitchen a few times, but I really like it." He poured cream into his coffee.

"I like it too," she admitted as she filled her own cup. "It's always felt like a *real* kitchen to me. All that stainless and granite biz leaves me cold."

He nodded. "I hear you. I want to figure out how to ensure the integrity of my old kitchen too...but I want it to function. It's a bit of a dilemma." He set his briefcase on the kitchen table. "Okay if I set up here?"

"That's what I had in mind."

Soon they were seated across from each other and Lane was telling her about some ideas he had for a new KidsPlay logo. "I want to design new T-shirts and things. A fresh campaign to get everyone excited about sports again." Emma got out a pad of paper and some pens, and before long she was shooting ideas at him. They talked and drew and tweaked and jotted down more ideas. All in all, it felt like a fairly inspired meeting, and they actually accomplished quite a lot. It was much more fun than her old job selling silly e-cards had been.

"You're really good at this." Lane glanced at his watch. "But I know I've used up far more than an hour of your time. And I promised to keep it to an hour. I'm probably keeping you from something else."

She shrugged. "The only thing I had wanted to do this morning, besides helping Nona, was to pick up the painting I bought at the fundraiser." She tore off the last page from the notepad, handing it to him. "I know we're supposed to get them picked up today—and I'm working at the bookstore this afternoon."

"Why don't I give you a ride over there?" he suggested. "I have a couple of pieces I need to pick up myself."

"Okay." She glanced at the kitchen clock. "That'll give me time to get back here and get Nona's lunch started."

It wasn't until he was parking the car in front of the Hummingbird that she realized this could be a fresh invitation to trouble. Surely, Anne would be working. She wouldn't like seeing them coming in together. But then Anne knew they were having a business meeting this morning...so really, why should she care?

"Well, look who's here," Anne said as Emma walked in. "And you brought Lane with you."

"Or Lane brought me," Emma said. "I want to pick up my painting."

"Oh, yes." Anne smiled at Lane. "And you have some pieces too, don't you? Let me tell Wendy to go find them for you. We're anxious to get them out of here and get this place back to normal. People have been picking them up all morning."

Anne disappeared and Lane turned to Emma. "I know I said it before, but I still marvel that you and Anne are sisters. You're so different."

"Dad says that Mom and Anne got the French, English, and German genes. He and I are products of Nona and Poppi."

He nodded, smiling as Anne and her assistant returned with the paintings. "Did you really buy this one?" Anne asked Emma. "Seriously? On purpose? Or did someone twist your arm?"

Emma reached for the seascape. "I bought it because I really like it."

"Oh, Emma, you're such a sentimentalist. Well, at least you donated your money to a good cause." Anne chuckled as she reached for the next painting.

Emma gazed at the seascape in her hands. She knew Anne was putting her down, and her sister's words stung, but she would not deny she liked this piece—even more in the daylight. "I've always believed that art, like beauty, was in the eyes of the beholder," she said quietly.

"Yes, yes, to each his own." Anne laughed as she handed Lane an attractive still-life painting. "Now, this guy, on the other hand, has exhibited some very fine taste in his selection of art." Anne winked at Lane as if they were sharing a secret joke. But the expression on Lane's face was unreadable.

"That *is* a nice painting," Emma agreed. "But I still like mine better."

Anne frowned down at the seascape, pointing to the signature. "I don't even know who this Randolph Lawrence is, since this was dropped off when I was out, but I'm guessing it's some old dude who decided to give up his paint-by-number sets." She giggled.

Lane cleared his throat. "As a matter of fact, I painted this."

Emma stared at Lane. "You're kidding."

"No." He gave her a sheepish smile. "Although after hearing your sister's opinion of my talent, I might be wise to keep my mouth shut on the matter."

*"Oh, Lane!"* Anne's hand flew to her mouth. "I'm so sorry. I had no idea." She pointed at the signature. "But that's *not* your name." She cocked her head to one side. "You're punking me, aren't you?"

"Not at all," he said solemnly. "Randolph is my middle name. Lawrence was my father's name. I suppose I was trying to slide this painting under the radar." He gave Emma an apologetic smile. "And if you'd like your money back, I'm perfectly glad—"

"No way!" Emma clutched the painting even tighter. "I love it and I am not giving it up."

"Oh, Lane." Anne put her hand on his shoulder, looking up into his eyes with a horrified expression. "I'm so sorry...and now that I look at the painting, it's really not—"

"No worries, Anne. I don't plan on giving up my day job anytime soon." He turned to Emma. "Don't you need to get back to fix Nona her lunch?"

"Yes!" Emma nodded eagerly.

Anne followed them to the door. "Emma," she said urgently, "before you go, I need to ask a favor. Can you watch Tristan for me on Thursday night? There's a Chamber meeting." She pointed to Lane. "You're going too, aren't you?"

"It's on my calendar," he told her.

"Anyway, if you could watch Tristan—"

"Sure." Emma smiled at her. "I'd love to. Have him stop by the bookstore after school and I'll take him home with me."

"And could you drop him at the condo...so he can go to bed?" Anne glanced at Lane. "You know how late those Chamber meetings can go sometimes."

"No problem," Emma said as she and Lane stepped out the door.

Anne was still walking with them, reminding Emma of a little terrier chasing after the mailman. "I am sorry, Lane," she continued. "I hope you'll forgive me. You know how I sometimes speak without thinking." She giggled. "I really need to work on that."

"It's okay, Anne." He opened the back of his SUV and put the paintings in. "I've never taken my art seriously." He laughed as he closed it. "And now I see why."

Of course, this made Emma feel bad, but she tried not to show it as she opened the passenger side.

"Wait, Emma," Anne called out, hurrying over to her. "I've been thinking you and I have not really had a chance to catch up since you've been home. I thought maybe we could do lunch tomorrow. Are you free?"

"Sure." Emma nodded.

"I'll fix us something special at my condo," Anne warmly told her. "Is noon okay for you?"

Emma agreed as she and Lane got into the car then he drove away in silence. "Did that bother you?" she asked him. "I mean, what Anne said?"

He chuckled. "I'll admit it was a bit awkward and I was tempted to keep my mouth shut about the whole thing." He glanced at her. "But that seemed unfair."

"I stand by my opinion," she stated. "I like the painting. And I'm not saying I know more about art than Anne, but I did take a little art in college and I enjoyed attending gallery exhibits in Seattle. I'm not exactly an ignoramus when it comes to art."

He laughed. "No, I doubt you are."

On Tuesday, Emma felt uneasy as she knocked on her sister's condo door. Besides the fact that Anne had never been a good cook and usually preferred to eat out, something about this lunch date felt suspicious.

"Welcome," Anne said brightly as she opened the door. "I picked us up some salads at the deli." She nodded to some cartons on the breakfast bar. "Hopefully you'll like the selection. I realized after I got there I should've given you a call."

"No, that's okay." Emma removed her jacket, laying it on a bench by the door. Anne chattered as they filled their plates then took them over to the dining table.

"Oh, these roses take up so much room." Anne slid them to the other end of the table. "But they are beautiful."

Emma nodded. She didn't really like roses that much, but they were very elegant-looking. "They look perfect in here," she said. "Very sophisticated."

"Do you know that Valentine's Day is just a week away?" Anne forked into a salad.

"Yes, Nona and I were just talking about that this morning."

"How is Nona?"

"She's okay. I mean, she gets blue occasionally, and I've caught her crying a few times. But she's keeping busy. And today her widow ladies are coming over for lunch—Lucille and Esther. That'll be nice for her."

"That's good. I keep meaning to stop by and visit... but it's been so busy."

Now Emma told Anne about how their dad was taking secret cooking lessons from Nona. "Don't tell Mom. It's supposed to be a surprise."

"That's precious. Nona teaching Dad to cook." Anne laughed. "Too bad Mom doesn't want to learn too."

They chatted amiably like that for a while and Emma decided that her earlier suspicions were completely unfounded. Anne had simply wanted a sisterly luncheon for them both to catch up. And it was kind of nice not being in a restaurant too. Anne went to get seconds on the turkey and apple salad, pausing by the roses to take a long sniff. "I know these aren't going to last much longer, but they're so pretty. I wonder if I should dry them, you know, for a *keepsake*. Do you think they'd dry nicely?"

"Maybe. You might try hanging them upside down, but don't let them get too wilted before you do."

"Good idea." Anne sat back down, looking directly at Emma. "Speaking of the lovely roses... I wanted to talk to you about Lane."

"Lane...?" Emma poked her fork into her pasta salad.

"Yes. I'd like to have a little heart-to-heart talk."

"Uh...okay..."

"I know that Lane's been quite friendly to you, Emma. And I think that's very sweet on his part. I just don't want you to get the wrong idea from him. You know what I mean?"

"Not exactly." Emma took a bite and chewed slowly.

"I mean I understand how Lane is a very attractive bachelor in our small town, Emma. It's only natural that he's caught your eye." She laughed. "He catches a lot of eyes. And he's such a friendly guy...to everyone...well, it's possible that you've misunderstood his intentions. You know?" Anne peered curiously at her.

"You mean because we did some marketing work together?" Emma said innocently. "Because, don't worry, that was purely business."

"Yes...I get that." Anne narrowed her eyes slightly. "I guess I should just get to the point, Emma. Lane has been an important part of my life for some time now. And for Tristan too. Tristan absolutely adores Lane."

"I know. I saw them together on Saturday. It was obvious that they're close."

"And so you see, there is something in the works here...something I'd like my sister to respect." Anne pushed her plate away with a serious expression. "I didn't want to say anything, but Mom mentioned that she had to tell you this same thing, Emma. She was worried that you had misunderstood Lane's friendship with you. She said that she explained that he's on good terms with the *whole* family." Anne sighed happily and gazed at the roses. "And we all think that's because he is hoping to be *part* of this family. With Valentine's Day just around the corner...well, I wouldn't be a bit surprised if Lane decided to take our relationship to the next level, if you know what I mean."

Emma's appetite vanished as she nodded. "Yes, I think I know exactly what you mean, Anne."

"I didn't want to be quite this blunt with you," Anne stood, picking up her plate and carrying it into the nearby kitchen. "But after talking to Mom, well, it just seemed the direct route was the best route. You know?"

Emma stood too, carrying her own plate to the sink. "Thank you for lunch, Anne. And thank you for being so honest with me."

"So you will respect my boundaries?" Anne locked eyes with her. "And Tristan's?"

"Of course. Why wouldn't I?"

Anne smiled. "See, that's just what I told Mom. She was all worked up over nothing."

Emma took in a deep breath. "I really should go, Anne. I promised to work at the bookstore. It's been busy there with Poppi gone."

"Yes, yes. I need to get back to the gallery too." Anne reached out for a hug. "Thanks for being so understanding, sis. I knew you would."

"Uh-huh." Emma couldn't think of an honest response that she was comfortable saying. "See ya 'round."

"And don't forget Tristan on Thursday," Anne called out as Emma pulled on her jacket. "Those Chamber meetings can run late...maybe even eleven. Is that okay?"

"It's fine." Emma reached for the door. "See ya." As Emma left, she felt a plethora of emotions—everything from outrage to betrayal...but mostly she felt hurt. As if her mom and sister had ganged up against her, and it cut to the core.

# Chapter 11

For the next day and a half, Emma tucked the conversation with her sister into the recesses of her mind. With so much else going on, it wasn't difficult to be distracted. Between helping Nona and working at the bookstore, her days were fairly full.

"Emma," Virginia said urgently on Wednesday afternoon. "Can you cover for me tonight? Tom's mother just went into the hospital with a heart attack, I'd really like to go see her, but I'm scheduled here until eight."

"Why is the store open tonight?" Emma asked.

"It's a book club night," Virginia explained. "Tonight is men's night."

"A men's book club?" Emma was surprised.

"Poppi got it going a few years ago." Virginia was checking her iPhone. "It was slow starting, but it's caught on. About a dozen men are involved."

"That's wonderful, Virginia. And I'm happy to stick around. Anything I need to know?"

"Not really. The men handle the book club themselves. But with the store lights on, sometimes customers will pop in. And someone might want coffee. But you know how to work the machines now. And if you wouldn't mind cleaning them out before you go home. That's about it."

Emma assured Virginia she could handle it, then called her mom to be sure that she'd be home with Nona. "Do I need to go home early?" Saundra asked. "Because I'm with a client right now and it could go until sevenish."

"That's fine," Emma told her. "Nona already has something for dinner." She restrained herself from saying that was perfect since her dad was having a cooking lesson tonight. So now she called her dad's cell phone and told him that he could linger longer than usual if he wanted tonight. "Mom won't be there until around seven."

"Great. Then Nona and I can actually eat my cooking lesson...well, if it's edible." He sniffed loudly. "It's smelling pretty good though."

"You're making me hungry," she told him.

"I'll leave you some leftovers," he promised.

"Why aren't you part of the men's book club?" she asked.

"You know...I kept thinking I'd get around to it. I promised Poppi I would. I guess I should look into it."

"Yes," she urged him. "You should." Then she thanked him for saving some leftovers and hung up. The bookstore got quiet after Cindy and Virginia were gone. Emma figured everyone was probably home fixing dinner. But the lull in business gave her a chance to tidy things up, and she even put on the Dean Martin CD, humming along as she spruced up the lounge area, where the book club was supposed to be held. A couple of lone men were wandering the store, and she suspected they were part of the group. Possibly they were concerned that Poppi would be missing tonight. Hopefully they wouldn't get discouraged and go home.

Although that seemed unlikely. Especially since the bookstore was so cozy and homey at night. What a lovely way to spend an evening. Perhaps she'd join a book club herself. Remembering that Valentine's Day was around the corner, she decided to treat the men readers to a nice box of chocolates from her Valentine's display. Opening the box, she even put some lace paper doilies beneath it and set it in the center of the coffee table. Perfect.

She was just dropping the plastic wrapper into the trash can when she heard the bell on the front door tinkling. Looking up, she was surprised to see Lane coming in with a bag in his hand. "Emma!" he exclaimed happily. "I didn't expect to see you here tonight." He came over and set the bag down. "You joining the men's book club?"

She laughed. "No. But I was thinking I might join the women's club. Or perhaps even start up a mixed group club, if no one's done that yet."

He grinned as he unzipped his parka. "That sounds like fun. I know I'd come."

"So are you part of the men's book club?"

He nodded. "Yep. And with Poppi gone, I thought I'd even offer to lead it tonight. Unless someone else steps up."

"So Poppi led it?" she asked sadly.

He hung his coat over the back of a chair. "Yeah . . . and he's pretty much irreplaceable. But hopefully we can slog through without him." He pointed to the chocolates. "You do that?"

"Yeah. You know, since it's almost Valentine's Day. Seemed kind of appropriate."

He set a book on the table and she peered down to see. "*Phantom of the Opera?*" she asked in surprise. "Really? Is that your book tonight?"

"Poppi insisted on a romance book for Valentine's Day," Lane said.

"Kind of a strange romance, don't you think?"

"I wasn't too sure about it at first. And the guys did some whining and complaining last month, but Poppi promised that there would be some action and intrigue. And he was right. It was a good book. I enjoyed it." Lane was unloading some things from his grocery bag: a prepared cheese plate and box of crackers, as well as a veggie plate and a plate of heart-shaped cookies with red and pink sprinkles.

"Very festive," she told him. "Does the men's group always get such fine treatment, or is this just for Valentine's Day?"

"The guys come here expecting some goodies. Poppi had them trained." He folded the grocery bag, tucking it under his arm as she removed lids and things from the food. "But Poppi usually provided it, and it was always much better than this since he and Nona did the cooking." Lane looked uncertain. "You think this will be okay?"

"I think it's perfect."

"Well, not quite perfect. We still need to open a bottle of red wine and get the glasses, napkins, and plates."

"Can I help?"

He gave her a grateful smile. "I was hoping you would."

As they walked to the back room together, she felt her heart doing its little flip-flop routine again. Why did he do that to her? Now she was assaulted by a rush of guilt as she remembered Anne's heart-to-heart talk the other day. But it's not like Emma was initiating anything. Was she? Still, just recalling her sister's words was painful. And confusing.

"I can't believe I'm feeling nervous about tonight," Lane said as they carried the things back to the lounge area.

"Oh, I'm sure you'll do fine."

"I don't know about that." He set a couple of opened bottles on the table. "Your grandfather is a hard act to follow."

"He did love his books," Emma admitted as she set the plastic cups on the table. "It was how he perfected his English."

"I know. He was extremely well read, and his vocabulary was impressive."

"Nona always felt like Poppi had the advantage over her." Emma laid the napkins out in a little fan design. "Because Poppi's father was a Lutheran pastor."

"I know," he said again. "I was a bit surprised to hear that. You usually assume all Italians are Catholic." He stepped back to view the table, nodding with satisfaction.

"Yeah, just having the name Burcelli, I've explained quite a few times why I'm not Catholic."

"Poppi told me about the persecution his family suffered during World War II because of their religious beliefs. I never realized that was going on."

"What's that?" Emma was surprised.

"Didn't he tell you?"

"About being persecuted?" She shook her head. "No. I realize many of his relatives, including his father, died in the war. But he never spoke of it much."

"They were hard stories to speak of...but Protestants in Italy were not very popular. And Lutherans in his town, after the war, were associated with Nazis."

"Really? He told you that?"

"I think he needed to talk."

She was trying to absorb this—her grandfather's family

had been persecuted for their religion. It just seemed so strange...and strange that she'd never heard about it. "But I remember hearing stories about how Poppi's parents tried to help and protect Jewish friends. They got a number of Jewish families safely over here."

"Yes...but apparently the Burcellis had enemies just the same. Some people choose to hate simply because of differences."

"That's so sad."

The bell on the door tinkled now. "Ahhh." Lane waved to the two men coming into the store. "The fun is about to begin."

"I'll get out of here," she said. "I'm sure they don't want to see a woman around."

"Don't worry." He winked. "Once the men get to talking, they're pretty oblivious as to who is listening."

Just the same, Emma busied herself behind the coffee counter. She had noticed that the entire area looked due for a good scrub-down, and since there didn't seem to be any other customers in the store, she decided to attack it. However, since the lounge was nearby, it wasn't difficult to overhear parts of the conversation. To her amusement, there were mixed feelings about the book and some of its characters. About midway through the discussion, and after the coffee machines and counters were clean, she sat down on the stool and, pretending to be reading on her iPad, she listened.

"Erik was a disingenuous bully," a man declared. "Someone should have killed him the first time he kidnapped Christine."

"And then there'd be no story," Lane pointed out.

"Erik wasn't disingenuous," an older man argued. "He

made it perfectly clear that he loved Christine and would do anything to win her."

"Including holding her against her will, even though he knew she loved Raoul?"

"But Raoul was a wimp," a young man said.

"Was he weak or was he just trying to be understanding?" Lane asked.

"That's right. Raoul knew that Christine cared for Erik."

"And don't forget Erik helped her with her career."

"But that doesn't make him a hero," the young man said.

"And forcing her to marry him—that was all wrong."

"He didn't force her," Lane said.

"Well, he coerced her. And she was willing to marry him, out of pity."

"Poppi thought this was a love story," Lane said evenly. "What do you guys think—is it about love?"

"It's a story about unrequited love," an older man said. "But not true love."

"But Erik truly loved Christine," someone said.

"Did he love her? Or did he just want to own her?" Lane asked.

"And what about Raoul? He loved her too. In the end, it's Raoul who gets her. Is that the love story?"

They kicked this around for a while, and it was amusing hearing men talking about love and romance. In some ways they seemed even more candid than women might be. Or perhaps it was the wine talking. Several bottles were opened now.

"You know what I think," Lane said with finality, and Emma's ears perked up to listen. "I think that every woman has a phantom in her closet."

The men laughed and made a few jokes.

"What do you mean?" the young man asked.

"Well, maybe not *every* woman," Lane clarified. "And to be fair, let's not limit my statement to women. I think most people have a phantom in their closet."

"Can you please explain that," the older man said.

"Think about it . . . have any of you had someone who has loved or admired or even been obsessed over you? At any time in your life?"

It was quiet for a bit, but then most of them chimed in, admitting that was true. "And it feels rather flattering to be the object of someone's affection, doesn't it?"

Again they agreed.

"And don't you think most people dream of loving and being loved like that?"

Again they agreed.

"But what if the illusion of the phantom kept people from risking themselves because they were afraid they wouldn't experience the measure of love and romance that they so desperately longed for? What if they closed the door to love?"

"Is that what the story was about?" someone asked.

"I don't know for sure," Lane admitted. Now he laughed. "I guess I was just hoping to come up with a great line . . . the way that Poppi used to do."

"Well, that was pretty good," someone said.

"And I know people like that," the young man added. "I won't name names, but I have a female friend with a phantom in her closet."

They laughed and made light of this. But as Emma considered Lane's words, she couldn't help but wonder if they were aimed at her. Although it was ridiculous, not to mention narcissistic, since he couldn't even see her where she was sitting tucked away behind the cappuccino machine.

Eventually the meeting broke up, and after the last of them

left, she went out to help Lane clean up. "Sounds like you guys had a fun evening," she said as she gathered up paper plates and napkins, dropping them into the plastic trash bag she'd brought out.

"Were you listening?"

"Some of the time. But I didn't hear everything."

Lane held up a bottle of wine. "There's a couple glasses left in here. Want to finish it off?"

"Unless you've already had too many." She peered curiously at him. "You have to drive, you know."

He laughed as he filled a plastic cup. "Don't worry. I limited myself to one. I wanted to stay on top of things as the leader tonight." He handed it to her.

"Did they like having you as leader?"

"They seemed to...although I couldn't begin to replace Poppi." He filled his own glass then held it up to her. "To Poppi?"

She nodded, touching the plastic cup to his. "To Poppi. I think he would be proud at the way you handled the book group tonight."

They sat down and she asked him some more questions about the Burcelli family history in Italy, listening and sipping her wine as he told her some of the stories Poppi had told him. "As sad as those things were," he finally said, "it's a wonder that Poppi was such an eternal optimist."

"But he was, wasn't he?" She smiled to remember her grandfather.

Lane nodded, looking at his nearly empty wine cup. "Poppi always saw the glass half full...even when it looked like this." He finished his wine and stood. "I guess we better get this place cleaned up so you can go home, Emma."

She didn't want to go home. However, she knew she

couldn't say that. Especially after her conversation with Anne yesterday. And the memory of those red roses and Anne saying how much Tristan loved Lane and how Anne expected their relationship to rise to the next level soon...perhaps by Valentine's Day. "Yes." Emma stood and continued gathering things up, wiping down the table, and soon she was turning off lights and they went outside and she locked the door.

"No ice escapades tonight," Lane said a bit sadly.

She peered up at the sky. "It's clear as can be."

He looked up too. *"When the world seems to shine like you've had too much wine, that's amore!"* She laughed to hear the words to the old Dean Martin song and joining with him, she sang as he walked her to her car. "Goodnight, Emma," he said warmly.

As she tried to say goodnight, a lump filled her throat as if she were about to break into tears, which seemed totally silly. And so she simply waved and got into her car.

# Chapter 12

The next morning, Emma's dad showed up at eleven for what he said was the final cooking lesson, although Nona disagreed. "Tomorrow's the big night," he told Emma as the three of them stood in the kitchen, watching as he carefully cut out raviolis. He was trying to increase his repertoire.

"Big night for what?" Emma asked.

"He's going to kidnap your mother from work tomorrow," Nona explained.

"And I'll take her home with me and cook spaghetti and meatballs," he told Emma. "Do you think it'll work?"

She suddenly remembered what Lane had said at the men's book group. "I think it could work, Dad. After all, every woman has a phantom in her closet."

"*What?*" Rob and Nona said simultaneously.

She laughed. "Everyone wants to be loved fully and completely, and I'm sure that's all Mom wants too."

"How better to love than with spaghetti and meatballs,"

Nona concluded. "As long as you make it with good Italian sausage and ground veal and minced garlic and sweet onions." She smacked her lips. "And sun-dried tomatoes and virgin olive oil and red wine and lots of fresh basil and oregano."

"Sorry I can't stick around and sample your cooking lessons today," Emma said, "but I am needed at the bookstore."

As she walked to town she wished she'd taken the time to talk to her dad about the situation with Lane...and Anne's recent heart-to-heart. But she didn't really want to have that conversation in front of Nona, because she didn't want her to feel stressed that there was any trouble between the two sisters. Nona used to warn them whenever they would bicker as girls that "bad blood between sisters was the worst thing that could happen to a family." Emma didn't want Nona worrying about that now.

The bookstore was fairly quiet in the afternoon, but with Virginia gone again, spending a couple hours with her ailing mother-in-law, Cindy and Emma managed to stay busy enough. And when Tristan showed up after school, Emma asked him if had homework, and he claimed that he didn't. "So have you done your valentines to give out at school yet? Did your teacher give you a class list?"

"Yeah...but that's girl stuff," he proclaimed.

"*Really?*" She peered curiously down at him. "So you don't like it when you get valentines? You'd rather no one gave you any?"

"Well..." His brow creased.

"Because if you don't give anyone a valentine, it seems selfish to expect them to give you any. But it might be embarrassing to be the only kid in your class who doesn't get a single valentine next Tuesday."

Now his eyes got wider. "Well, I guess maybe I should give out valentines too," he admitted.

"And we did have a nice selection over there. Although a lot of kids from your school have been buying them lately, so it might be getting limited." She pointed to the table. "Why don't you pick some out and you can sit down and work on them in the lounge. Need some cocoa to go with the job?"

He nodded eagerly, hurrying over to peruse the various boxes and packets of cards. And before long, he was hard at work, with his list spread out in front of them, carefully writing them out.

At five o'clock, she and Tristan went home and, thanks to her dad's cooking lesson that morning, they had leftover raviolis for dinner. Naturally, Saundra assumed that Nona and Emma had made them earlier, and no one said anything different. Still, Emma couldn't help but be amused to think that her mother would be kidnapped to her own home tomorrow night... and to her husband's cooking. Emma had been praying that it would go well. Not just because she and Nona were weary of having Saundra living here, but because she knew her parents belonged together. She just wished they knew it too.

"Time to go home," she told Tristan after they finished cleaning up the dinner dishes. "Gather up your stuff." Soon they were on their way, and she could tell by how quiet he was that Tristan was either tired or worried.

"You okay?" she finally asked as they walked up to the steps to the condo.

"Yeah..." He said a bit sadly.

"Really? You don't sound okay to me." She waited as he fumbled to find his key in his backpack and then unlock and open the door. "You sound like something is bothering you," she said as they went inside.

He shrugged, dumping his backpack and then his jacket onto the floor.

She kneeled down and looked into his face. "Did I do something to offend you?" she asked with concern.

He shook his head. "No. It's not you, Aunt Emma."

"What is it?"

"I...uh...I miss my dad."

"Oh." She nodded, slowly standing. Then, placing a hand on his shoulder, she walked him to the living room. "Want to talk about it?" She sat down on the sectional and he sat down beside her, fidgeting with a hole in the knee of his jeans.

"Dad called me a couple days ago," he began.

"Uh-huh?"

"He just wanted to talk and stuff."

"What do you guys talk about?"

"He asks me about school and playing basketball. Just regular stuff."

"Do you enjoy talking to him?"

"Yeah." He nodded eagerly.

"But it makes you miss him?"

He let out a long sigh. "Mom doesn't like it when he calls. She got mad at him last time."

"Why did she get mad at him?"

"For talking too long."

"Oh..."

"She said from now on we can only talk for ten minutes."

"Oh..." Emma grimaced.

"And that makes me miss him even more."

"Do you want to talk to him right now?" Emma asked.

"Yeah!" he said hopefully.

She pulled her cell phone from her purse. "You know his number?"

"Sure."

"Well, go for it. I won't tell if you don't tell." She handed him the phone. "But you have to promise to end the conversation by your bedtime, okay?"

"Okay!" He was already dialing her phone.

Emma knew she was probably overstepping one of Anne's boundaries, but she didn't care. After all, Anne had entrusted Tristan to her care, hadn't she? She hadn't given any real instructions. What was wrong with Tristan speaking to his dad?

Emma picked up a slick fashion magazine and leaned back into the sectional, absently flipping through it until she got tired of seeing one expensive ad after another—all seemed to be for diamonds or chocolate or vodka or beauty products. She looked at the front to see it was a February edition. Or course, the magazine was capitalizing on Valentine's Day. She set the magazine down, listening to the lilting sound of Tristan's voice as he chatted with his dad. He was telling him about how Aunt Emma made him do his valentines today. But she could tell that he wasn't really mad about it.

Finally, she realized that it really was close to his bedtime and he hadn't even put on his pajamas or brushed his teeth. She went into his room and pointed to her watch. "Sorry, Trist, but time's up."

"I gotta go now, Dad. Yeah, that's Aunt Emma. Wanna talk to her?" He told his dad goodnight and that he loved him then handed the phone back to Emma.

"Hey, Gerard," she said in a friendly tone. "How are you doing?"

"Great, thanks. The job is really working out. It won't be long until I can get a transfer."

"Really? Do you think you could move back here?"

"I hope so. I won't know until June."

"Oh, Gerard, that would be wonderful."

"I'm glad you think so. I wish your sister felt the same."

"Oh . . . well, Tristan would sure be glad to know this. Have you told him?"

"I hate getting his hopes up. He's already counting the days until spring break."

"I know. That's so cool you're taking him to Disney World."

"I wish Anne would come with him. I don't really like the idea of him flying all that way alone. And I told her that there'd be no strings attached. She could stay in a hotel and do her own thing and enjoy some Florida sunshine while Tristan stays with me."

"That sounds like a great offer. Anne loves the sun."

"Yeah . . . but she refuses to come."

"I know."

"Any chance you could talk her into thinking about it?"

"I doubt it." She walked through the kitchen, running her hand over the sleek cold granite countertop.

"So you think she's really finished with me then?"

"I don't know, Gerard. To be honest, I don't really get it."

"No . . . I don't expect you do. Sorry, Emma, I shouldn't trouble you with my problems."

"That's okay, really. If I could do anything to help, I would."

"And if you had any suggestions, you'd let me know?"

"Absolutely."

"The roses obviously didn't work."

"Roses?" She looked at the dining room table, staring at the red roses, which were starting to wilt.

"Yeah. Dumb idea. I sent her two dozen red roses on the anniversary of our first date back in high school. She never even acknowledged them. Probably threw them in the trash. I almost asked Tristan, but didn't want to make him feel bad."

"Actually, she kept the roses, Gerard."

"She did?" His voice brightened.

"Yeah...they're on her dining room table right now."

"Hmm...maybe there's hope."

"I don't know, Gerard. But if it's any consolation, I've been praying for you two to get back together. I know that's what Tristan wants too."

"Thanks, Emma. You're a rock. And thanks for letting Tristan call me on your phone too. I know that Anne has limited our calls to ten minutes. The judge wouldn't agree with that, but again...I don't want to rock her boat."

"I told Tristan I wouldn't mention this call to his mom."

"I get ya. Thanks."

They said goodbye, and Emma went over to the roses that had supposedly been from Lane. Oh, maybe Anne hadn't said as much, but she had certainly insinuated it. And, seeing the dark red petals on the table, she no longer felt guilty for overstepping any boundaries with her sister. Not when it came to Lane Forester anyway.

Maybe this was childishness on her part, or maybe she was stooping down to Anne's level, but Emma was fed up. Of course, she was well aware that her baby sister had always been a master of manipulation. Whether it was by batting those big blue eyes or stomping her little size six feet, Anne knew how to get what she wanted. She'd been doing it all her life. And maybe it was about time Emma put a stop to allowing her little sister to work her.

The next afternoon Lane came down into the bookstore. At first Emma thought he was just passing through, but then she noticed he appeared to be looking for something on the Valentine's Day table.

"Can I help you?" she asked cheerfully.

"Oh, Emma, I didn't see you there." He set down a leather-bound gift edition of *Pride and Prejudice* and smiled at her.

"Looking for a valentine for someone?" she asked. Suddenly she wondered if he was picking out something for her sister. And if he was, wouldn't she feel foolish for asking to help? Perhaps she should just leave.

"As a matter of fact, I am." He looked directly into her eyes.

"Well, as you can see, we have an assortment of gift suggestions." She knew her voice sounded overly formal and businesslike, but she couldn't help herself.

"I know. That's why I came here. I need something really special."

"Well, a good book and a good box of chocolates can be pretty special."

"These leather-bound Austen books are very nice." He picked up *Emma*. "Particularly this title."

She laughed nervously. "Yes, well, that's an exceptional Austen book. Many think it was her best."

He nodded. "I'd be inclined to agree."

"You've read it?"

"Sure. Poppi encouraged me to sample Jane Austen along with all the other classics."

"My mother loves Jane Austen," she confided. "Anne and I were both named after Austen characters."

He nodded. "Poppi mentioned that to me once." He tucked the book under his arm. "And which chocolates go best with this particular title?"

She frowned down at the chocolates. "I don't know. It depends on who you're buying them for. Some people like dark chocolate. Some like light. And some even like white." She wrinkled her nose. "Not me."

He chuckled. "Me neither."

"I think this box looks like a good one." She pointed to the most expensive box of chocolates. "Although it's mostly dark chocolate and someone like my sister would be disappointed because she hates dark chocolate."

He picked up the box. "That looks perfect."

Now Emma felt a small rush of hope going through her.

"I saw the sign on the door saying that you ship Valentine's gifts, but today is the deadline for getting them there in time."

"That's right." She nodded, feeling idiotic again. Had she really assumed the book and chocolates were for her? What was wrong with her? "Want me to wrap it and get it ready for shipping?" she asked. "UPS picks up in about an hour."

"Yes. You get it started while I pick out a card."

"Certainly," she said in her formal tone again. "I'll get right to it." Feeling like a romantic fool, she walked over to the register, where she carefully wrapped the book and chocolates in pink tissue paper, topped by a pretty foil paper with red and pink hearts. She also took the time to put a ribbon around it, carefully curling it. She was just finishing up when Lane came with a card.

"That looks pretty," he said as she rang up the purchases. "My mom is going to love it."

"It's for your mom?" she said wistfully. "How sweet."

He locked eyes with her. "Yeah, I think she'll like it. Especially the book title."

Emma didn't know what to say to that. More and more she felt like she was on a roller-coaster ride with this man. Up and down and up and down. She waited as he filled in the address information then signed the receipt and gift card. "That's all we need," she told him. "The UPS guy should be here before long and it will get to your mom by Monday or Tuesday at the latest."

"Thanks." He continued standing there, with both hand palms down on the counter, just watching her.

"Anything else I can help you with?" She glanced over his shoulder to where an elderly woman was waiting with several books.

"As a matter of fact, you can." He made a hopeful smile. "Let me take you to dinner on Saturday night."

She blinked. "What?"

"I'm asking you out, Emma. Will you go?"

"Well...uh...yes." She nodded eagerly. "I'd love to."

*"Really?"* He looked shocked.

"Yes. What time?" She smiled at the woman.

"Uh...is seven...uh...okay?" He still looked surprised, almost as if he thought she'd decline.

"Perfect."

"Great. I'll pick you up at seven then." He grinned. "See ya."

On Saturday morning, Emma was a bundle of nerves. To think that she was going out with Lane tonight. But she was trying to act calm for Nona's sake.

"I guess Dad's dinner was a success last night," she said as she set a bowl of hot oatmeal in front of her grandmother.

"What makes you say that?" Nona looked up with interest.

"Mom never came home." Emma filled Nona's coffee cup. "I mean back here. I assume she slept in her own bed last night."

Nona chuckled. "Praise be to God."

Emma got her own bowl of oatmeal and sat down, waiting for Nona to say her usual blessing. Then, as they quietly ate together, Emma told Nona that she had a dinner date. "We have still have leftovers from cooking lessons with Dad," she said. "But I can fix something—"

"No, no." Nona held up a hand. "I put up with this when Saundra was here, Emma. But now that it's you and me, I want you to stop coddling me like an invalid."

Emma smiled. "You're not an invalid."

"I am feeling strong and well, *dolce*. Yes, I am sad sometimes. But when you love someone as I loved Poppi, you have a right to be sad, no?"

Emma nodded. "Yes, Nona. You have a right."

"Now, tell me. Who is your dinner date? Is it a man?"

"As a matter of fact, it is a man." Emma took in a breath. "It is Lane Forester."

Nona's dark eyes lit up and she clapped her hands. "Oh, *dolce*, that is wonderful."

"Really?" Emma was almost afraid to breathe. "But what about Anne?"

"What about her?"

"I think she's in love with Lane."

Nona waved her hand dismissively. "Does not matter."

"Why not?"

"Lane is not in love with her."

"How do you know?"

"You just look at him, *dolce*. You can see it. Poppi knew it. So do I."

"But Mom thinks they should get married. Anne does too."

"Does not matter what they think. Lane knows what he

wants. He has asked you to dinner, *dolce*. That is all you need to know."

"But what about Anne? What about bad blood between sisters?"

"Oh, *cara mia*. I think you worry too much."

Emma smiled. "I think you're right."

"You know what Poppi would say, don't you?"

"Follow your heart?"

Nona patted her hand. "Yes. And not to worry so much! It is much better to pray than to worry, *dolce*."

"I'll try to keep that in mind." And throughout the day, that is exactly what she tried to do. Each time she felt worried, she prayed. And by the time she was getting ready for her date, she felt relatively relaxed.

# Chapter 13

Emma knew it was a little redundant, and her mother would certainly not approve, but she dressed in the exact same outfit she'd worn for the fundraiser for Saturday night's date. But when Lane picked her up, he told her she looked beautiful and she could tell by the look in his eyes that he meant it.

"Thank you," she said as he opened the car door for her. "You look very handsome too." Although Lane wasn't dressed formally, he looked smart in his dark trousers and well-cut suede jacket.

He thanked her, and she took in a steadying breath as hurried around to his side of the car. She couldn't believe she was really doing this—having dinner with Lane Forester. It seemed like a dream.

"I'm so glad you agreed to go out with me," he said as he drove toward town. "For some reason I was certain you were going to turn me down when I asked you."

"Why?"

"A number of reasons."

"Such as?"

"For starters, you told me yourself, the night we decorated the bookstore, you were soured on romance."

"Yes, but I'm trying to adjust my attitude."

"Besides that, it seemed each time I thought we were getting somewhere, you'd chill me out or shut me down. I couldn't figure you out."

She pressed her lips together. "Well...that had to do with Anne."

"You really believed I was interested in her?"

"I wasn't sure how you felt, but I knew she was interested in you. She still is." Emma exhaled loudly. "In fact, when she hears about this...well, it will be awkward."

"I'm sorry, Emma. Have I put you in a tough position?"

"A little bit."

"But Anne will forgive you, won't she?"

"I don't know...I hope so."

"She will, Emma. I know she will."

"Yes...you're probably right."

"For the remainder of the night, I want to make one rule. If you don't mind?"

"What's that?"

"We will not talk about or think about your sister. *Okay?*"

She made a relieved sigh. "Yes."

"Now I want to know more about you," he said as he turned onto Main Street. "I want to know *everything* about you."

"Everything? All in one night? You must think there's not much to tell," she teased.

"Well, hopefully we'll have more than one night to get acquainted. But tell me about yourself, what it was like growing up here, your college days, your job in Seattle, your ex-boyfriends." He chuckled. "I want to hear it all."

So as the evening progressed, Emma told him about how she often felt the misfit as a child. "At least in my own family. Mom and Anne were like two peas in a pod. I really related more to Nona." She described her college days, which sounded rather uninteresting. She even told him how she got her heart broken once and how most of the guys were just plain disappointing.

"Although I think I might have a phantom in my closet," she confided as he parked the car in front of the elegant Napoli Restaurant on top of the hill overlooking the town.

"So you *were* listening the other night."

She laughed. "Well, my phantom is probably different than what you were suggesting. But I think it messes with my mind just the same."

He went around to her door, reaching for her hand to help her out. "Did I tell you that you look beautiful?" he said in a slightly teasing tone.

"Yes, I believe you did. But don't hold back—feel free to express yourself."

He chuckled. "Well, you *are* beautiful, Emma. And it feels good to be able to tell you. I wanted to say so before, but I wasn't sure you were ready to hear it."

She laughed. "I've never felt beautiful," she admitted as they walked up to the restaurant. "I always felt like the ugly duckling growing up. Anne was the beauty."

"Like you said, it's in the eyes of the beholder." He opened the door to the restaurant. "Do you like Napoli's?"

"I adore it."

"I thought you would. Some people think it's old-fashioned, but I love it."

Before long, they were seated and their conversation continued. But after a bit, Emma told him it was his turn to answer questions.

"Yes, of course. Ask away. I have nothing to hide."

"Good...so do you mind if I cut to the chase?"

"Please, do."

"I've asked myself dozens of times why a great guy like you is still single. If it's not presumptuous, will you please explain yourself?" She smiled hopefully.

"Absolutely." Lane started in on a story of how he'd been equally interested in sports and academics in school. "I was kind of shy around girls in high school, then I got a college scholarship, as a result I took my studies seriously. Then I was very focused on my career and building a business. I was too distracted to do much dating." He gazed fondly at her. "Besides, I was waiting for the perfect girl."

"Me too," she declared. "I mean, the perfect guy. Everyone told me I was setting my sights too high."

He pointed to his chest. "Same thing. When I turned thirty, my mom started a gentle nagging campaign. She was worried I'd never find someone. About that time I met a beautiful woman...Brianna. And I suppose I was ripe to become totally smitten. A bit like poor Erik in *Phantom of the Opera*. I was beside myself with her beauty...so much so that I completely forgot to investigate her character or get to know her better."

"Oh..."

"By then I was working with my business partner, a guy named Marcus—who was married with a baby on the way—and, well, we were pretty well established in our software design firm. Had some really good accounts. In other words, we were successful. So Brianna and I married, and I thought we were happy, or I told myself we were happy. She seemed happy. We had a nice home, good friends. But I did work a lot. Anyway...two years into the marriage, I found out that she was having an affair."

"Oh, no." Emma shook her head.

He nodded. "She was sleeping with Marcus."

"Your partner? But he was married? With a child?"

"All of the above."

"Oh...dear."

"That's when I decided I'd had enough. I made the knee-jerk decision to sell my half of the business to Marcus. And I left Seattle and Brianna to take this job here. Last I heard, Marcus's marriage bit the dust and he and Brianna are still together. I just hope Roxie—that's Marcus's first wife—got a good settlement from him."

"So that's why you were a little jaded about love and romance when you moved here?" she said slowly. "Why Poppi took you under his wing."

Lane chuckled. "I can't help but think Poppi was grooming me."

"For Anne?"

He shrugged. "Or for you. Who knows?"

They talked on and on, enjoying the food and the company and the wine. But finally Emma felt concerned for Nona. "I hate for this evening to end," she said. "But Nona is home alone." Now she told him about how her mom had gone back to her dad yesterday.

"Well, that's good news. But you're right. We should get you home."

They continued talking all the way home, and she considered asking him in, but wasn't sure about it. And so when he walked her to the front door, she simply thanked him. "It was a perfect date," she told him. "Beyond anything I ever imagined."

"Then let's end it on a perfect note." He leaned forward. "If you don't mind."

"Not at all," she whispered as she leaned toward him. Suddenly she felt herself melting into a kiss that was so full of passion and warmth and longing that she felt slightly breathless and weak in the knees.

"Perfect," she whispered as they stepped away.

He nodded. "Perfect."

On Sunday, Emma rose early. She felt as if she were walking in a sweet dream as she fixed her and Nona's breakfast and then got ready for church. However, as she drove into the church parking lot, she was not so sure. What about Anne and Tristan? Didn't Lane usually sit with them in church? How would Emma feel if he was doing that today? Why hadn't she asked him about it? She still had so many questions.

She waited as Nona slowly made her way out of the car, then, linking her arm in hers, they walked up to the church. They were about halfway there when Lane came out to meet them. Falling into step alongside Nona, he took her other arm in his. "Good morning, ladies," he said cheerfully. "Can I escort you into the sanctuary?"

They thanked him and he led them in, and then the three of them sat in Nona's favorite pew. As the church filled up, Emma tried to ignore the looks that she got from Anne as well as her mother, who was sitting next to her dad. Fortunately her dad just smiled and waved. And once again, instead of worrying or obsessing, Emma decided to simply pray.

After the church service, as they visited with her parents,

Tristan came over to talk to them. To her relief, he seemed completely oblivious to what was so obviously disturbing his mother. Anne was standing a fair distance from them, pretending to visit with a friend, but her eyes kept darting toward them, and the expression on her face was not a happy one.

However, Lane and Emma continued acting perfectly natural, as if there were nothing unusual about them being together. And soon they were exiting the church with Nona. Emma let out a big sigh of relief. "Glad that's over," she said as they walked through the parking lot.

"Well done," Nona told her. "And Anne will get over this. Probably much sooner than you expect."

Emma wasn't so sure, but was glad it was over, and when Lane invited them to join him for lunch, Nona gladly agreed. Lane asked Nona to choose the place, and she told him that she wanted pizza.

"Then you shall have pizza," he assured her. As he drove to Nona's favorite pizza shop downtown, he started to sing. "When the moon hits your eye like a big pizza pie..." Emma and Nona joined in. *"That's amore."*

On Monday, Emma still felt like she was walking on the clouds. Lane had visited her at Nona's house the night before and then called her again that morning, just to say hello and that he was thinking about her. Emma couldn't remember when she'd ever been so completely happy. Well, except for the Anne thing. That was the proverbial fly in the ointment. However, she was determined not to worry. She could imagine Poppi telling her to pray instead. And that was exactly what she was doing.

However, as she worked in the bookstore all afternoon, she

had the distinct feeling that a confrontation was coming, almost like she could see the dark storm clouds gathering—right across the street at the Hummingbird Gallery. Okay, the clouds were just her imagination, but it would be so unlike Anne to do nothing. Emma just hoped Anne wouldn't march into the bookstore and throw a nasty hissy fit with customers watching on. That would be such a sad scene—especially on the eve of Valentine's Day.

Because it was Monday, the bookstore closed at five. And since Virginia's mother-in-law was still in the hospital and Cindy had to pick up her daughter from ballet, Emma had offered to close up shop. She was so relieved when the last customer left at two minutes before five. Hurrying to the front door, she was just turning the lock in the door when she saw a chic-looking figure darting across the street.

As much as she wanted to pretend she hadn't seen her sister, turn around, and go back into the shadows of the store, she knew she couldn't. Instead, she turned the lock and opened the door, stepping aside as Anne came in. Once Anne was inside, she locked the door again. And she pulled down the shade. "Hello," she said cautiously. "You know that we're closed, but I suspect you're not here to buy a book."

"You got that right." Anne glared angrily at Emma.

Emma picked up a UPS box that had been delivered earlier, carrying it toward the back room and silently praying. She could hear the quickly clicking heels following right behind her. "I can tell you're upset," Emma said as she set the box on a work table.

"Of course, I'm upset. In fact, upset doesn't even begin to describe it." Anne slammed her designer purse on the table next to the box. "I am furious, Emma. I am enraged at you. And I have every right to be enraged."

*"Every right?"* Emma tilted her head to one side. "Can you explain that to me?"

"Oh, yes," Anne seethed. "That's exactly what I plan to do. I cannot believe that you, my very own sister, have betrayed me like this, Emma. I lay my heart before you, I tell you what's going on, and you sneak around and stab me in the back."

"Wait a minute." Emma held up her hands. "How did I sneak around and stab you in the back?"

"I told you all about Lane and me. You knew that we were together. I warned you that you needed to back off, but did you listen?"

"What do you mean you *were together*, Anne?" Emma's hands were shaking, but she kept her voice calm.

"We were a couple, Emma. You *saw* us together— numerous times. And you know how close Tristan is to Lane. You could see what was going on here. And Mom told you to back off too. But did you listen? Did you?"

"But I—"

*"Listen to me now!"* Anne shouted. "You betrayed me, Emma. You swooped in here and proceeded to try to steal my boyfriend and—"

"That's not true."

Anne narrowed her eyes. "Maybe it's not true yet. Maybe you haven't actually stolen him yet, Emma, but you've been trying. And just so you know, I'm going to fight you on this."

"But, Anne, you don't understand. Let me—"

"I do understand, Emma. I understand that you are a lying, cheating, backstabbing, sorry excuse of a sister. And I hate you!"

"Anne . . ." Emma pressed her lips together. "How can you say—"

"I have been working on this relationship for two years,

Emma." Anne shook two fingers in Emma's face. "I have invested myself completely in this relationship. I've been supportive of everything Lane's doing. I set up that fundraiser. And what about Tristan? If you don't care about me, what about your nephew?"

"I love Tristan," Emma said with tear-filled eyes. Anne's words were still tearing away at her inside. "And I love you too, Anne."

"If you love me, you will back off from Lane, Emma."

"But you don't under—"

"I understand this, sister. I've worked on this relationship for two years. And you're here for less than two weeks—and you think you can unravel all my hard work. Well, you might've turned Lane's head for a day or two—probably because you bought that ridiculous seascape, and I'll bet you knew what you were doing when you did. But, mark my words, dear sister, I will win him back. You'll see."

"Don't be so sure of that."

Both Emma and Anne turned at the sound of his voice—both were equally shocked to see Lane standing in the shadows near the stairs.

"I'm sorry to be eavesdropping," he said as he stepped into the light. "But I heard raised voices and was concerned. When I heard my name mentioned . . . well, I thought that was an invitation to join in." He walked up to Anne with a stern expression. "I considered you my good friend, Anne. *Nothing more.* I've tried to make that perfectly clear from the start. I've never asked you out once. I've never made a single advance. All I've offered you was my friendship. If you misread that as something more, I'm sorry."

Emma looked at Anne. Her eyes were wide and her face looked pale.

"I never meant to hurt you," Emma quietly told her. "But you deceived me, Anne."

Anne turned to look at Emma. "I deceived *you?*"

"You led me to believe that you and Lane were a couple. You insinuated that he'd sent you those roses. But they were from someone else. Someone who truly does love you, Anne. They were from Gerard."

Anne's mouth twisted to one side.

"I'm sorry you felt like you were investing yourself in a relationship with me," Lane told her. "I thought you were helping with the fundraiser and everything just because you cared about the kids and the community. And I'm sorry that I didn't realize that you wanted more than just friendship." Now Lane stepped closer to Emma, slipping his arm around her shoulders. "And I'm sorry if my feelings for Emma are up-setting to you. But I'm sure you'll get over this. Much sooner than you expect. Don't worry, Anne, you'll move on."

Anne snatched up her purse with angry eyes. "Well, maybe you two deserve each other," she snapped as she rushed out of the back room.

"Wait," Emma called. "I need to unlock the door for you." She hurried, catching Anne at the door. "I really am sorry I hurt you," she said as she fumbled with the key, getting it into the lock. "And if it's any comfort, I was holding back my feelings for Lane. It wasn't until I found out about the roses...how you tricked me...that I let my guard down." She clicked the lock open.

"*Whatever!*" Anne jerked open the door and slammed it so hard that the shade rolled up with a loud snap.

As Emma watched Anne storming away, she suddenly re-called one of the few times when she'd had the courage to cross her strong-willed little sister. Emma had been in high school, and one night when she was getting ready to go on a church hayride, Anne threw a horrible fit, saying it was unfair that the hayride was just for the high school kids. Anne was only in middle school at the time, so Emma refused to take her. Anne was so enraged that Emma felt certain she'd never get over it. But by the time Emma got home, Anne had two of her friends over for a slumber party and all was forgotten...although probably not forgiven. Hopefully Lane was right, Anne would get over this much sooner than she expected.

# Chapter 14

Early on Valentine's Day morning, Emma heard the doorbell ring and was surprised to find her dad at the front door. In his hands was a small bouquet of red roses and pink carnations. "These are for your Nona," he said quietly. "I don't suppose she's up yet?"

"I just heard her stirring." Emma opened the door wide. "Want to come in and wait? I already got coffee started."

"Coffee sounds good." He checked his watch. "I've got about thirty minutes before my first appointment."

After they were settled in the kitchen with their coffees, her dad admitted that he'd heard about the sisterly feud from Emma's mother last night. "I hate to say it, but I could see that one coming from miles away."

"I guess I should've seen it too."

"At first your mom was all worked up that you'd put the moves on Anne's man." He chuckled as he lifted his coffee cup. "But I set her straight on that one."

"Thanks." Emma took a sip.

"Anyway, your mom's happy about you and Lane. So am I."

"I wish Anne were too."

"Unfortunately, your sister doesn't seem to know a good thing when she has it, Emma. She's always been a grass-is-greener sort of girl, you know?"

With her eyes on her coffee, Emma just sighed.

"That's what happened between her and Gerard."

She looked up. "What?"

"Oh, no one will come out and say it, but I know it's true. More than thirty years of practicing law...a man learns to read people. Even ones in his own family."

"What are you saying, Dad?"

"Can you keep this between me and you?"

"Of course."

"Anne started getting chilly toward Gerard shortly after Lane came to town. Now I'm not blaming Lane, because I'm sure he didn't realize what was going on. Anne is brilliant at convincing people to see things her way. You know that as well as anyone."

"Yeah." Emma nodded emphatically.

"Suddenly Anne was finding fault every which way with Gerard. The poor boy couldn't do a thing right...in her eyes. But from what I could see he was a good provider and a good father. Tristan adored him. Still does."

"I know."

"But Anne was shutting him out, pushing him away. Naturally, that'll bring some strife into a marriage."

"But why would she do that if Gerard was such a good guy? I mean, I've always thought Gerard was a good guy. But why would Anne throw all that away?"

"My theory is that she believed she'd outgrown Gerard.

They were so young when they married, it makes some sense. Anne got the job at the gallery, and she suddenly felt very important. And I think she felt like she deserved someone more prestigious than an insurance salesman for a husband. She saw Poppi befriending Lane...and she decided he was just what she needed."

"Oh..." Emma thought about her conversation with Gerard. "Do you think there's any chance that Anne and Gerard will get back together?"

He shrugged. "Well, now that Anne's been knocked off her high horse...maybe."

"I know Gerard wants to make another go of it."

"I'd say his chances are better now than ever." He smiled at her. "Maybe you can help your sister think this whole thing through. I mean after she's had some time to cool off. You might be able to influence her a little."

Emma was just agreeing to this when Nona came into the kitchen. Dressed for the day, she greeted them both cheerfully.

"Happy Valentine's Day," Rob said as he kissed his mother on both cheeks. "I brought these for you."

Nona's eyes lit up. "Poppi always got me flowers for Valentine's Day. Sometimes it was just a single rose. But he always brought home something." Now her smile faded slightly.

"Well, you can just pretend that these are from both Poppi and me," Rob told her. "And now I better get to my office, or my client will throw a fit."

Shortly after lunch the doorbell rang again. This time it was a delivery man and for the first time in her life, Emma received flowers on Valentine's Day. To her relief they were not red roses.

"*Oh, my!*" Nona exclaimed as Emma carried the enormous

bouquet of multicolored tulips into the living room. "Are those from Lane?"

"Yes." She'd already read the card, which simply said, *To Emma, Love Lane. I will see you tonight.* "Aren't they beautiful?"

"Oh, my, yes." Nona smiled. "It feels like springtime just to look at them."

"I'll put them right next to your bouquet for you to enjoy." Emma set them on the marble-topped table by the front window. "In a way these are partially from Poppi too," she said as she pulled on her coat.

"But they are from Lane. How can they be from Poppi too?" Nona asked curiously.

"Poppi was a mentor to Lane. It was Poppi who helped Lane to believe in love and romance again," Emma explained.

Nona nodded. "Yes, I know all about that."

Emma leaned down to kiss her cheek. "Don't forget that your lady friends are coming for the tea party at four. Make sure you get yourself a nap before they come...so you won't be worn out."

Nona smiled and waved. "Yes, yes. And I know where the food is that we fixed last night, Emma. *I am fine.* You go to work and do not worry about me, *dolce.* And let's not plan on dinner tonight. I won't want more than a piece of toast by then anyway. Happy Valentine's Day, *cara mia*!"

"Happy Valentine's Day to you too, Nona."

Emma's feet felt light as she walked to town. Today was going to be a good day. She knew it. However, when she turned onto Main Street, she felt a trace of sadness to see the Hummingbird Gallery across the street. Unfortunately, Anne was probably not having a very good day. Not that there was much Emma could do about it.

The bookstore was in good spirits. Cindy informed her that

business had been brisk all morning, and Virginia's mother-in-law had been released from the hospital and was expected to make a full recovery. Even Gattino looked festive with a red bow around his neck.

"Will you take the Valentine's decorations down tomorrow?" Cindy asked her.

"Oh, I don't know...." Emma sighed as she gazed up at the colorful hearts and cheery cupids. "There isn't any hurry, is there? I kind of like seeing them up there."

"Sure," Virginia said. "Why not leave 'em up?"

Tristan came into the bookstore after school, and, as usual, Emma treated him to a cocoa. "I got lots of cool valentines," he told her as they sat down at the table by the window. "Wanna see?"

"Sure do," she said as she sipped her latte.

One by one he took them out, explaining who had given him each one. As he chatted happily, she kept an eye out for a certain tall handsome guy. But to her dismay Lane had not made one appearance in the bookstore this afternoon. However, she wasn't worried. She felt certain she would see him before long. At least by tonight, according to the card with her flowers.

"Those are some very cool valentines," she told Tristan as he stuffed them back into his pack. "Thanks for showing them to me." Now she got an idea. "Did you give your mom a valentine yet?"

His brow creased. "No. Should I?"

"Yes, of course, you should."

"I don't have any money to buy anything."

"That's okay. We can find her something here. I'll help you with it."

So after he finished his cocoa, they went over to the valentine table and Tristan looked around, finally deciding on a box of chocolates and big musical card.

"Do you think she'll like this?" he asked as he signed the card.

"I know she will."

"I don't need to get her flowers," he said as he slid the card into the envelope. "Dad sent her a great big bunch of roses. Pink ones this time. That's her favorite color too."

"Really?"

"Yeah. And she was so glad about the roses that she let me talk to Dad for more than ten minutes last night. I talked to him for about thirty minutes I think."

"*Really?*" Emma felt incredibly hopeful.

"Uh-huh." He paused in licking the sticky part of the envelope. "And Mom told Dad that she was thinking about going to Disney World too."

"Oh, Tristan, that would be wonderful if she went with you."

"I know." He nodded as he sealed it closed. "I'm praying that she will."

"Me too," Emma promised. "I'll be praying too."

"Should I take this to her now?"

"You bet," she told him. "And give her a big hug and a kiss too. I have a feeling she needs it today."

He wrinkled his nose then nodded firmly. "Okay, Aunt Emma, *I will*."

Emma watched as he hurried out the door, looking both ways before he crossed the street. And as she watched, Emma kept her promise and prayed.

Lane arrived just as she was closing up the store. "I had to go to Seattle for a special Big Brothers Big Sisters meeting today," he explained as he hugged her. "Did you get my flowers and my message about tonight?"

"I did. Thank you."

"Well, I tried to make us a dinner reservation in town," he said as she locked the door with them still inside. "But all the good restaurants were booked until around nine. And I knew with Nona, you wouldn't want to stay out that late."

"That's true." Grateful that he understood, she told him about Nona's Valentine's Day tea party that she and her widow friends were having right now.

"Good for her." Lane unbuttoned his coat. "So, unless you think it's a bad idea, I thought maybe we could have a little Valentine's Day dinner right here tonight."

She looked around the cozy bookstore. "Really? Right here?"

"Do you mind?"

"Not at all. I love this place." She waved her hand. "And look, it's all decorated."

"By some real pros too." He grinned. "Dinner won't be fancy tonight. But I did order some things to be delivered. Is that okay?"

"That's perfect," she told him. "Food is really secondary to company."

He embraced her again. "See why I love you?"

She blinked. "Did you just say what I thought you said?"

He nodded. "I do love you, Emma Burcelli." And now he kissed her and it was even more wonderful than the first time.

Her heart was pounding hard, but she knew what it was telling her. "I love you too, Lane," she said quietly. And they kissed again.

"I knew that I loved you the first time I saw you," he said as he ran his fingers through her hair.

"Really? When was that?"

"Well, the first time was at Poppi's funeral service. I knew who you were right away. And I could hardly take my eyes off you."

"You knew you loved me then?"

"Well, I probably wasn't calling it love yet. But you had my full attention."

"You caught my attention that day too... when you spoke about Poppi in the church. I was really touched. But then I heard you belonged to Anne... my balloon was burst."

"If I'd only known you'd believed that. It was never true, Emma. Not in my mind anyway. What a mess this all could've turned into." He shook his head. "So the next time I saw you was at your parents' home. Did you know that I was watching you?"

"You were watching me? I thought I was watching you."

He laughed. "I saw you interacting with guests, being so helpful, so caring, so genuine... I tried not to be obvious, but I couldn't take my eyes off you."

"That's so funny. And I was trying not to feel jealous of Anne because I believed that you guys were a couple."

"But it really sealed it for me when I found you sitting with Tristan in your parents' sunroom. I could tell you were trying to encourage him and I know he was really hurting. And I could tell whatever you were saying to him was working. You seemed so sweet and sincere and beautiful."

"You thought all that back then?"

"I did. But it seemed like every time I tried to make a connection with you, you would hold me at arm's length. I started to think that you really didn't like me."

"That was because of Anne."

"I know."

Now Emma told him about what Tristan had said about the pink roses.

"Hope springs eternal," he said as he touched her cheek.

"But I want to make a rule for tonight," she said quietly.

He just nodded. "Yes, I agree. We won't talk about or worry about your sister."

"Thank you." She smiled. "I am praying for her though."

He glanced at his watch now. "The food should be here soon, but I'm guessing they're busy because of Valentine's Day."

"Even if no food comes," she murmured, "I won't complain."

"See why I love you?" He kissed her again. "Well, if the food doesn't get here we'll just feast on wine and chocolate," he teased.

"What are we waiting for?"

"You're right! You get the chocolates and I'll get the wine."

"Don't forget Dean Martin," she told him.

"Happy Valentine's Day, Emma."

"Happy Valentine's Day, Lane."

As they hurried off to get their provisions, Emma knew it was going to be the happiest of Valentine's Days ever. Romance and love were not dead after all—they never had been. As she heard the happy strains of Dean Martin singing "That's Amore," she felt certain that Poppi was smiling down on them right now. And as she hurried back to the lounge area, where Lane was waiting with a big bright smile and a pair of wine glasses, she knew that this was simply the beginning of a lifetime of Valentine's Day celebrations to look forward to in the future.

Melody Carlson is the prolific novelist of more than two hundred books with more than six million copies sold. She has won numerous honors and writing awards, including the Rita, the Gold Medallion, the Carol Award, and the *Romantic Times* Career Achievement Award. Melody has two grown sons and makes her home in the Pacific Northwest with her husband and their dog, Audrey. When not writing, Melody enjoys biking, gardening, and camping in the beautiful Cascade Mountains.